To: D[...]

More [...] friend.

that el [...] ever [...] Fun, energetic, supportive and a great mom. Glad to know you.

Love Ya,

Let

An Urban Greek Tragedy

It Go

Sean Cleveland (signature)

Sean M. Cleveland

Outskirts Press, Inc.
Denver, Colorado

Let It Go
An Urban Greek Tragedy
All Rights Reserved
Copyright © 2007 Sean M. Cleveland
V2.0

Outskirts Press
http://www.outskirtspress.com

ISBN-13: 978-1-4327-0747-7

Outskirts Press and the "OP" logo are trademarks belonging to Outskirts Press, Inc.

Printed in the United States of America

Introduction

"Niggas do not love us. Don't let none of these dudes that's out here telling you that they love you, they want to take care of you and want to be with you forever fool yo ass. That's all bullshit. All niggas love is getting they Dick sucked and pussy. Niggas love to fuck. And they'll fuck you however you let them and they'll fuck any bitch that's giving it up, whether they claim that they love you or not. If you a chick a guy will let you suck his dick and will run up in you. Ugly, pretty. fat, cute whatever it don't matter to a nigga with a hard on. They don't give a fuck. It's all about ass, so I figure fuck it. He getting what he wants, so I should get that new purse, them new shoes or that cash for the club. He get to run up in it, so I should get to run up his credit card. " Joy said to her girlfriends."

As you can see Joy is just a little on the abrasive side, with a whole bunch of attitude. She is like so many other young Black women of this now generation, who feel that happiness is spelled (L-E-X-U-S or M-O-N-E-Y). They also seem to believe that babies are trophies or status symbols of some kind. And like their older counterparts from long gone generations, they always appear to equate sex with love. So if a man fucks you really well, it means that he loves you or cares very much. And as a man, I can tell you that that particular thought is not always true. Most time's pussy is just pussy.

She was born Joyana Brown, daughter of Stephanie and whoever the Daddy is Brown, on 11-25-81 in the Jersey City Medical Center. Her and her mother lived on the Woodward Street side of the Lafayette Gardens housing project. Her mother named her Joyana because she felt that her daughter was the only good thing that she had ever accomplished. Obviously she did not conceive her on her own, but she would have to raise her alone. This was mainly her own fault since she couldn't honestly be sure of whom the father was. That fact secretly bothered her very much. Deep down inside she had always been ashamed of her money driven promiscuity, but couldn't seem to help herself. Sex was the only thing that produced any kind of pleasure in her life. It was the only thing that made her feel good, until her Joy was born.

She thought to herself that existence would be different now. Life would be magically filled with substance and meaning. At first it was true and it did happen like that for them. Joyana brought Stephanie the first true happiness that had ever entered her life. She felt joy. However, the happiness of their new lives would be short lived. Circumstance would do what it always does and turn their lives upside down. Despair would come to her in many different forms.

Let It Go

The Start of it all

Stephanie was sitting on a bench beneath her window when she met Slide. He was tall and slim with a devilish smile. The fellas gave him this name because of the way his left leg strategically slid with each delayed step. He was too cool for his own good.

"Hey lady what's up? How you doin'. The fellas call me Slide. So, what's your name?"

"I'm Steph and I know who you are. I've seen you sportin' yo ride." She said in a matter of fact tone.

"Oh, yeah my Beema (B.M.W). You like her color: candy-apple red." He said proudly, while smiling at his ride lovingly. "That's my chick. She takes very good care of me."

"Umm, hum, I bet she do. You be getting' yo swerve on up in there don't you. Sliding' around on those leather seats wit them heffas."

"Nah. Brotha man right here does not get down like that. I have respect for women and for my wheels. I can't be riding around havin' my shit smelling like a fish market. That mess ain't fly."

The whole time she was smiling from ear to ear at the fact that this fine and paid young man (with an emphasis on the paid part), was trying to kick it to her even though she had Joy. However, Steph should have been able to read his mind or at least been a better judge of character. Because had she been, maybe his obviously dangerous edge would have shown in the sunlight, before it had a chance to cause any wounds. Regrettably, all she saw was the pretty face, the pretty, expensive car and his size thirteen shoes. The pretty face meant that she could flaunt him to her friends. The pretty and expensive ride meant that she could travel in style and profile. And with her fingers crossed, she hoped that his size thirteen's meant that his 'thang' was big.

Slide was digging' her too. Why wouldn't he? Especially since she was cute, fair skinned and stacked. Steph was five feet five inches tall, with round, bouncy size 36c's and one of those fat ghetto booties, that stopped traffic when she crossed the street. Even after having recently had a child, Stephanie had it goin' on. Slide was definitely interested. And the fact that she had a child was a plus, because to him (and also 93% of today's men), it was a clear sign. A young woman with a child is like a red light for most men in terms of having a relationship with the woman. But if a relationship is not in the plans, it's probably the biggest, brightest green light a man gets to see now a days. It's like she has a sign on her head that says " an easy piece of ass." So the first thing that we men do in a situation like this is test the water. We want to feel the woman out and see just how vulnerable she is and just how much of herself she's willing to sacrifice in order to get a father figure for her child. That's exactly what Slide was wondering the first time that he saw her.

"Honey got a kid. That's real cool. So I don't have to wait for that stuff." He thought to himself as he drove into the parking lot, on the Johnston Avenue side of L.G.

"If her kid's pops ain't around, then I'm gonna try to hit that. Shit, I can picture that ass now, bent over and bouncing while I try to kill it. Umm, Lovely."

Now here he is face to face with all of them titties plotting her conquest. To him, Stephanie was just another trophy to go home and brag to the guys about. Slide was listening really close to her every word. He had to or how else would his keen vulnerability detector be able to detect the chinks in her armor?

"So what's the kid's name?" He said.

"Joyana." She replied.

"That's different and kinda fly too. Where's your man at? Is he around or is he one of them dudes that make 'little people' and bounce? You know them fellas with no hearts or sensitivity. See me, the Slide, I'm responsible. I take care of all three of my little monsters. I buy they gear, pay they school money and feed they little greedy behinds. I see them and their mommas once or twice a week, 'cause I'm a good pops." Slide boasted with a huge grin on his face.

Stephanie sat there smiling and staring at the handsome, financially secure and hopefully well-endowed man standing in front of her. It didn't seem to matter to her that he had three children, from what sounded like three different women. All she saw was the potential for some excitement to come into her life. Never once did it even dawn on her to consider the fact that he was an obvious playa, who collected panties like little boys collected bottle caps. All she wanted to do was fuck the really pretty man and maybe get some monetary perks in return. Her plan was to use what she had to get what she wanted. Sadly enough that seemed to be the attitude of the time, for both the men and women. The young males want all the sex that they can get from as many trophies as possible, while the females give of themselves completely in exchange for what they consider to be a taste of luxury and improved status among their friends. It's a strange game that human beings play with one another. It's a kind one-up-manship contest. Whose game is better and whose sex is stronger? However when viewed objectively, by this onlooker, there don't seem to be any true winners.

The women lose their respectability, their freedom and often times their identity and get very little in return. What ever it is that they get from the connection with the man they choose to deal with is fleeting. Purely temporary, because he either takes it all away as quickly as it was given, or it dissolves in her emotional waterfall. Meaning that she begins to love him without it being reciprocated. The cars, the clothes and the perks are all that there is. It's not the magical relationship that was imagined. It's more of a business deal. With a contract that if you had read the fine print carefully and noticed that your heart was the price to be paid, you may not have signed. And in the end, nine times out of ten, she's left holding the pieces of her heart and a child or two in her hands.

Today's young people don't seem to think about the consequences. The idea that every new relationship has the potential to fulfill, nurture, hurt, or destroy. When not taken seriously, these connections can result in any one, if not all of the three "D's": diapers, depression and disease. It seems like, 7 out of every 10 times, young men become runaways, (runaway fathers) and young women are forced to become the heroines of dramatic lives. Lives that can either be happy, sad, romantic or tragic, depending on the whims of chance and circumstance. All too often love begins for the wrong reasons giving it no real opportunity to sustain itself. Almost as quickly as it begins, it becomes tainted or contaminated. Resulting in a mutated version of what it should have been. Our youth has the tendency to look for love through open pants and open legs, instead of open eyes and open minds.

Stephanie Brown talking to her friends about her and Slide getting down

"Steph, that nigga Slide is fine and plus he got cash. I here that nigga got bank." Keyla gushed. Keyla is the member of the click that sees a man through money green glasses. If he has the cash he can have some ass is her motto. As a result, drug dealers, like Slide are her men of choice.

"Yo, ya'll know Sekena, from Montgomery was fucking that nigga right." Interrupted Cherry. "I hear that he don't eat coochie, but his stuff is fat and he can use it. So you better get some of that thang girl." As you can hear, Ms. Cherry James is a notorious freak that only cares about how much manhood a guy has strapped between his legs. Every man has a chance to take her to bed and if he can get her off, he can have as much of her as he can handle.

"Keyla, all you think about is doe and Cherry yo momma gave you the right name, since your cherry is all you ever think about. You got dick on the brain girl. Me, I need something different for a change. I want a nigga that's nice to me all of the time, not just when he wants his thang sucked or some of my stuff either." Said Steph.

"Hold up, tramp, did you just finally admit that you suck dick." Cherry said, "After calling me a hooker when I told ya'll that I love to give my nigga head. You is a lying ass bitch."

"You better check that shit right now hoe, 'cause I don't suck dick like you." Steph screamed, "I said that I don't want a man who just wants to fuck me and have me suck his dick all because he got loot. I need some love and respect from someone who will be a father figure to Joy.

"Well if you want a brother to stay with you, then you better suck his shit better than the next chick will and that's the motherfucking truth!" Cherry twisted her extended finger in the air as she gave this defiant piece of sexual advice.

"That's not true. A good man will stay with you because he loves you for who and what you are, not just your body." Ask Morece.

"Ask me what?"

"Does a good man stay with a woman just because she's fine and gives head?" Steph said looking at her only truly trustworthy friend, Moe.

Moe was the only guy that Steph ever trusted. He was the only reason that she believed that there actually were good men in the world, who cared about a woman's well-being, just because he did. He was tall, sensitive and sweet. Plus he had passed every test and spoiled every trick that she could think of to see if her body was his real objective. She walked around in front of him half-naked, gave him opportunities to kiss her and even pretended to be dead drunk. However, Morece was a real man, who really respected women as people. He would turn away when she wasn't descent, hug her and kiss only her cheek when she was hurting and vulnerable, and when she was pretending to be drunk, all he did was stretch her out on his couch take off her shoes and bring her a blanket. To her he was everything that she wanted in a man. However, Moe had no real flashy style or any money to burn. To her he was the safest place in the world. When she was around him any and everything seemed possible.

(Moe) "It would depend on your definition of a good man. What exactly do you need a man to give you in order to be happy?" Said Mo with slight hesitation.

(Steph) "No. Tell these heffas what you told me. What you think a real man is. What you've always tried to be like. Tell them." Steph urged.

(Moe) "Well, I feel like this. A man hears what you have to say and asks questions if he doesn't understand. He also gives the same respect to his woman that he feels is deserved by him. A real man faces up to responsibility head on, even when the odds are overwhelming. Most importantly of all, to me anyway, real men raise their children and do not use the ones that they love as punching bags."

The young ladies looked at him as if he was from another planet, or had two heads. They heard every word that Moe said, but it was obvious that none of them could relate to any of them. It's like I always say. You can lecture a person and spoon-feed them your life's tragic history or beautiful dreams, but none of those matters. That is because people are hardheaded and stubborn. Experience has to be their teacher and pain their guide. They have to live and learn. And hopefully, with every one of their good-byes they learn something.

(Steph) "Ain't that the sweetest shit you ever heard? Don't ya stuff just get all moist and shit? Well I do. That's the nigga I wanna meet."

Moe thinks to himself, that Stephanie met that man ten years ago, when they first bumped into one another. But he's always known that she'd never be his, since his pockets aren't that fat. Since day one, he's known that she was shallow and that it would be her downfall. He wished that he could change her, but knew better. You're better-off loving people as they are, because you can't actually change them on a truly fundamental level. Nine times out of ten you experience a superficial change that disappears as quickly as it came. So, you should stick around and hope for the best. That's what Moe decided to do, in the hope of helping her grow as a person. And maybe even help her to fall in love for real, (with him or someone deserving).

(Cherry) "That shit ain't real. Moe just like every other smooth talking brotha. Nice until you fall for his ass and let him run up in it. Then the nigga forgets how to be polite and all of that other sensitive shit. And you can believe that. That's why I'm just like the fellas. Out to get my shit off." Cherry said with a matter of fact tone.

(Keyla) "I don't give a fuck what nobody say. All every muthafucka that I met ever wanted to do was fuck me. Including my fucked up uncles and bitch-ass stepfather. His punk, broke ass been tryin to hit this since the day I got these big ass titties."

(Mo) "Damn, Keyla. That's messed up. That's not right. Have you told your mother about what he tries to do behind her back?"

(Keyla) "Naw. She love that sorry drunk nigga. But between me and y'all, if that nigga had cash and was giving it up plus buying me stuff, maybe he could get some." She said without flinching. However, everybody simply brushed it off. Everybody except Moe. It bothered him and made his stomach turn. To herself, she was thinking that if her mother's man was giving her money on a regular basis, it was his for the taking. Besides, he ain't her real daddy, so why not take advantage of a potentially lucrative money making opportunity.

(Steph) "Keyla, stop trippin'. You not that big a hoe. That shit would be so scanky."

(Keyla) "Fuck that, just like I said. Any nigga with enough cash coming out of his pockets and into my hands, can have as much of this 20-year-old ass he can afford. Why should I give up all of this fat, tight, pretty ass to some sorry brotha who swears to me that he loves me, but don't do shit for me? All he does is fuck me for free. Naw, you gots ta pay ta lay. Ain't no free rides.

(Cherry) "A nigga ain't gotta pay for my pussy. Even though, dinner, a movie and gifts will be asked for often. All a nigga gotta do for me is eat the cat and make me cum on the regular. Work his shit right and take me where I need to go. We straight if he can do that." Cherry said licking her lips.

(Moe) "Don't y'all want more than that? Don't the two of you need more than that? You know? Something real and touchable that you can hold on to?

(Keyla) "What the hell do we need that for? That love and sensitive brotha crap can't buy me dope gear, so forget that."

(Cherry) "Yeah, give me good sex over love any day."

Moe bit his tongue and kept his comments to himself. Sadly, he realized that these two young women had lived too much bad life too soon and couldn't get passed that. It would take some strong dedicated men or the hand of God to save them from their obvious, anger, pain and bitterness. Stephanie also worried about her friend and wondered if life would ever be good to any of them, (herself included). She wondered if any of the beautiful things that Moe always said were true. She wanted to know if any men other than him really felt any of those things that he talked about. Did they really know emotional pain and could they really be supportive and responsible when it mattered most? She had some serious doubts about all of that, but Moe was slowly convincing her otherwise.

(Cherry) "So Steph, you gonna give Slide some? You gonna let him feel it? Huh?" Cherry said excitedly almost as if she was getting off on the idea.

(Keyla) "Yeah Steph. You gonna give that nigga some play? Shit. Shake them titties in his face so you can sport that dope ride. Give up the ass for the cash. Hell, we can see you like that nigga. So what's the deal? What's up?"

(Steph) "Yeah, I like him. Besides he's fine as all

hell. Damn. Plus his beema is fly and he seems like a nice enough guy too. Don't he y'all?"
(Both girls) "Yup, that nigga is fine."

(Moe) "Hold up. Why are you two telling her to get with Slide for his cash?"

(Cherry) "No Moe. Not just the cash, the dick too. Ha ha ha. Never forget the dick."
(Keyla) "Nigga, you just mad. Everybody knows you want Steph's ass all for yourself. That's the only reason you keep filling her head with all of that 'nice nigga', Mr. Sensitive bullshit. Your ass ain't fooling me."

Before Moe could respond to Keyla's putting his feelings on the spot, Stephanie apologized to him and asked him to go, so that the three girls could finish their conversation. That way Moe and Keyla wouldn't bump heads, like they always seemed to do lately. Besides she could tell that he was a little sweet on her and didn't want to hurt his feelings. She loved him. However, probably not in the way that he loved her. She was sorry about that fact, and wondered what she could do to change things. Especially, since she didn't want anything to mess up their friendship. It was the most important thing in her life, next to her Joy. And as we all know, sex and physical intimacy have been known to ruin friendships. Stephanie wouldn't be able to handle such an occurrence, because she never wanted to lose Moe.

(Steph) " Key, why you always bothering him like that and giving him such a hard ass time? He's the nicest man, no the nicest person that I've ever met."

(Keyla) "So why you not sleeping with him, if he all a that? Damn, he cute, he got muscles and all of that sweet shit. So, why not fuck with him instead of leading him on?" Said Keyla defiantly, with a jealous tone.

(Steph) "I don't want to lose my best friend. And I am not leading him on for your information."

(Cherry) "Yes you is Steph. That brotha love you. He follow you around like a puppy and do everything for you. It's like you got him pussy-whipped, without even giving up the pussy. Plus, you know he want some and you won't give it up."

(Keyla) "Yeah, girl. You need to cut that shit out and stop playing with him like that." Keyla said almost angrily.

(Steph) "Hold up, woman. I thought that you didn't even like him. You sound like you do. What's up with that?" Steph said with more than just a little twinge of jealousy.

(Keyla) "I don't like him like that, but he is cool. Chicks be wantin' to talk to him, but they don't cause he's always around you. I just think that you'd be helping that brotha and yourself out if you cut him off and stop letting him think that he gonna get some. Especially, if you ain't gonna give him none, since he ain't got no real cash. That's all I'm saying. Fuck it. Forget that nigga anyway. What about Slide?"

Keyla hurriedly changed the subject, because she didn't want to give herself away. It would ruin her image with her girls if they knew that she had a schoolgirl crush on Moe. As a result she's been giving him a hard time lately in order to cover it up. Her infatuation with him grew because she knew for a fact that his kindness was real and free of charge. A few months ago, she bumped into him in their hallway, after having had a fight with her man of the day. She was in tears, so he took her to his apartment and let her cry on his shoulder for hours. He never once said a word. The man never pried into what had happened and never tried to take advantage of her vulnerability. And to top it all off, Moe made her dinner. The whole time that they were in his apartment, she waited for him to try and have sex with her, but nothing happened. The funny thing is that, Keyla probably would have given him some in the spirit of gratitude, but he never even tried to steal a kiss. At first she was offended and thought that maybe Moe didn't find her attractive. However, before she could get mad and curse him out for not attempting to fuck her while she was vulnerable, Keyla noticed something. Something that she had never seen in the eyes of a man before: kindness. Genuine one hundred percent grade a concern surrounded in compassion. She was caught completely off guard. It was the first time that a man had made her heart flutter without the aid of a gift. He was the first man that she had ever met. At least the first real man.

She would never forget his kindness and always remember what it felt like. Keyla believed that if she remembered it clearly enough, she might recognize it again if she ever saw it again. She's secretly had her fingers crossed and her heart open ever since.

(Steph) "Shhh, here he comes right now."

(Slide) "Hey, ladies, what's goin' on? Y'all just chillin' and kickin' it out here?"

(The girls) "Yeah, we hangin."

Just at that moment, little Joyana started crying. Her mother picked her up out of the stroller and reached for the milk bottle. It was empty.

(Steph) "Damn! I knew that I forgot to do something. Sitting here, cackling with y'all hens, I forgot to go to the store and get her milk."

Slide seized the opportunity and offered to take her to Path Mark. She accepted the invitation and the stage was set for that dramatic play that would change the rest of her life.

Slide and Steph start their relationship.

The inside of Slide's ride was just as nice as the outside. Stephanie was so excited, that her stomach was full of butterflies. After a while the excitement made her feel like she had to go to the bathroom and tinkle, but she held it.

She could not stop staring at him. He was just too cute. His smile was perfect and Steph loved the way that his pretty brown eyes reflected every light that they saw. She was ready for him, if he was a nice enough guy. She crossed her fingers and prayed for the best. Besides, Slide couldn't be too bad if he was doing her this favor for Joy.

It never once entered her mind that he might have ulterior motives. The thought never occurred to this naïve young woman, that her body was his objective. She was undoubtedly; blinded by the light that twinkled in his eyes. Stephanie was at Slides mercy from the moment that she entered his lair. She was being charmed, by a snake and didn't even see it coming. He had easily worked his pretty face having B.M.W magic.

Some relationships begin with flowers and some begin with friendship, while some catch you completely off guard blowing you away. Then there are those that begin with a dance or a kiss and there are also some that start with a bang like an explosion. Stephanie and Slide began their relationship with disrespect and disregard. All she wanted was a man with a little money, a little status and maybe a big penis, someone who could help ease some of life's burdens. A guy who would buy pampers, chauffer her around, keep her nails and hair done, while providing ample opportunity for her to floss and show off for her friends.

For two weeks it was lovely. Stephanie was treated like the queen of Slides universe. He played chauffeur, benefactor and wanna-be-daddy. He was definitely good at what he did. Because by the end of the second week, Stephanie was licking him like a lollipop, from head to toe with an extended stop in between. Slide had her so head over heels; that she was doing stuff to him that she swore to her girl friends would never happen. Regrettably though, the initial decision to expand her sexual horizons was not one that she made herself. It was made for her; just like so many of her other life choices would be, from that day forth.

(Slide)" You know I got a thing for you girl. So we goin to do this together thing or what?"
(Steph)" You wanna be my man? Is that what you mean?"

(Slide)" Yeah. You and me against the world, with Joy watching our backs. How dat sound?"
She smiled and blushed, surprised at the invitation of a relationship, but far from

hesitant. Never once did she even doubt the sincerity of his words. Not even when the first thing that he wanted from her was a blowjob.

(Steph)"If you for real, I'll be your girl. Why don't we go to Sizzler or something and celebrate?"

(Slide)"Sure, we could do that. But before we do lets lock up our commitment, ahight."

(Steph)"Like what? Should we jump up and down and shout it to the world at the top of our lungs. Nah, we should go to the liquor store and get a little something, so we can drink a toast to it."

(Slide)"Nah lets do something a little more personal and intimate. Gimme a kiss and show me all of that body you got under that dress, since you my girl and all."

Stunned. Stephanie hesitated and started to cuss him out, but stopped herself. She did not want to mess up a good thing and besides he seemed like a nice guy, so why not show him the goodies. Slowly, she reached back and undid her zipper, allowing her tiny dress to slip down on to the floor. There she was naked and standing in the middle of his living room, terribly excited and somewhat afraid. But Stephanie wanted him so bad that she felt it was worth putting herself so abruptly on display.

Besides that, the young woman hoped that he would take off his clothes too and give her some visual pleasure. However, instead of granting her secret wish, Slide began to touch her breast aggressively and pinch her always-perky young nipples until she squealed like a mouse. She loved the way that his hands demanded access to all of her secret places. It made her feel really nice and also made her smile. Stephanie wanted to return the favor, so she did. Her hand quickly found its way to Slides lap and down inside of his pants. It wasn't thirteen inches long, but it would definitely serve her purposes. The young lady was glad of that fact.

Suddenly without warning, a seemingly lovely moment took a drastic turn for the not so nice. Slide grabbed her by the back of her hair and forced her head down between his legs and shoved himself into her unwilling mouth. Steph gagged and nearly choked, but he wouldn't let her up until his mountain had erupted into her mouth. She didn't even complain. She never said a word (not that she could have at that particular moment anyway). All that the hurt and ashamed young lady did was swallow the evidence of her abuse and also her pride. Steph got dressed without saying a word and left quietly. He didn't even try to stop her from leaving or even ask what was the matter.

Once outside of the apartment, she began running down the street as if someone were chasing after her. As she ran wiping remnants of the thick liquid from her mouth, she looked back and wished that he had chased after her or at least asked her permission. She was so confused and disillusioned, by the pretty man and his actions. However, the entire time that she was running home, in her mind there was the hope that he would have a good explanation for ruining there first intimate moment. Even though somewhere deep down inside of herself she knew that the only real explanation for his actions was that he wanted his dick sucked. And that he did not respect her enough to ask, so he forced her. Sadly, instead of continuing to run in the opposite direction of Slide, she decided to stay and not let the pretty, well-to-do young drug entrepreneur, with the nice ride and the nice thang, get away. She figured that an occasional bad taste in her mouth wasn't that high of a price to pay.

Keyla and Moe's situation turns interesting

Steph didn't know whether or not she should tell her friends about what happened between her and Slide. But she did know that Moe could never find out about it. Even though it wasn't really a big deal for a boyfriend to want his girl to go down on him, she knew that her friend would get mad. First of all he would be jealous of the relationship itself. Because she was giving herself to Slide and not to him. Of course he'd never say anything to her directly, but his always-truthful eyes would tell on him. So she would only tell the girls, to see what they thought about it. So she could get someone else's opinion on whether or not she had over reacted. However after reviewing her choices of who to talk with, she decided against telling anyone what had taken place. It was her decision to be in the relationship, so it would be her cross to bare. She refused to bring her friends into her personal life any further than they already were. Besides, Moe would reprimand her or lecture her about how wrong it is for a man to disrespect a woman, and the girls would probably just look at her crazy, while wondering what the big deal was all about. She decided against telling any of them.

Stephanie was everything that Moe ever wanted. She was his be-all-to-end-all. He thought about her every moment of every day and smiled, but could never tell her to her face. It would be devastating if she laughed at him or shot him down.

(Moe)" If I tell her that I have feelings for her, will it change anything? Will it change everything? Will it even matter to her anyway? Does she already know how I feel? Will she be upset, or think that my kindness has always had an ulterior motive behind it? I don't know what to do or what to think. All that I do know is that seeing her draped all over Slide is killing me."

He hated it. Watching Steph play the role of trophy to a drug dealer, who would probably never love her. Who would more than likely, use her up and walk away. Moe really hated their relationship. It was breaking his heart. But even still, he vowed not to say anything to her out loud. He'd let her decisions teach her in their own time. He'd simply wait and hope for the best.

Ironically, while Morece was secretly pining over Stephanie, someone was fawning over him. Keyla could not help but wonder to herself, what it must be like to have a man love you. To have strong arms wrapped around you and broad shoulders to cry on. She desperately wanted to know what the word commitment really stood for and what it would be like to have an actual support system. To love someone who loves you, just as much and just because.

(Key)" He'd never want to be with me. He

probably thinks I'm a gold-digger or some mess like that. Why would he want used up merchandise? He knows how I am. Only after the cash in exchange for my company. But he has no real dough, so why am I flippin' like this over him? What can that bus riding nigga do for me?"

Keyla couldn't figure it out. She didn't understand what was going on inside of her. These were all new feelings to her. The young woman wondered how she could possibly be falling for a man without any money or status, even if he was kind of cute and really nice. All that she knew for certain was that she was starting to feel something and it was growing pretty fast.

Keyla runs into Moe late one night

The two were coming down the block from opposite directions, when their eyes met. Moe smiled, as if glad to see her, and then she returned the smile. They walked slowly toward one another like they were being drawn together.

(Moe)"Hey lady, what's up?" How are you doing?

(Keyla) " Fine, What's up with you? You just chillin by your lonesome."

(Moe)" Yeah. I didn't really have anything to do, so I figured that a walk would kill some time. Maybe find someplace quiet, stare up at the stars and be alone with my thoughts."

Keyla just stared up into his big brown eyes and listened closely to his every word. He sounded so nice to her. She could get used to hearing him say pretty things to her and maybe even about her too. Then out of the blue she did something bold: she touched his hand.

(Keyla)"Would you like some company? I mean, unless you really want to be alone and stuff. Cause if not, I'd like to go sit somewhere and talk if that's ah'ight." She couldn't believe that she said it, but she had. So she squeezed his hand and looked down at the ground, shyly waiting for him to answer. Her heart was pounding so loudly, that she could barely hear Moe when he responded.

(Moe) "If you'd really like to Keyla, it would be my pleasure to walk with such a pretty woman. I hope that I don't bore you to death with my company."

(Keyla)"You're not boring Moe. Different, but definitely not boring. I like the way that you talk and sometimes I wish that I could talk like you do. Then people might kinda take me more serious, you know." She said softly, while turning away from his gaze. "Let me stop. Before you think I'm corny or something."

(Moe) "Nah Keyla, you don't have to stop and I don't think that you're corny. In fact, I think that you're a really attractive young lady with a great deal to offer. You just need to give yourself some credit that's all. You know, be who you really are inside and not pretend so much." Keyla was stunned by the idea that Morece had paid enough attention to her to catch a glimpse of what was going on.

(Keyla) I don't pretend, not really. I might fake orgasm, but I don't fake what I like or what I want.

(Moe)"Ok. And I guess what you like are fancy clothes and cars and what you want is money."

(Keyla) Angrily Keyla asks,"Hold up, you trying to dis me and call me shallow."

(Moe)"Naw Keyla. I would never disrespect you for any reason; because you're my friend and friends don't do that to people they care about. I'm just repeating what you always say. "No cash, no ass, and no ride, no slide."

Keyla had to turn away from him, when he said those things. It hurt her so much to hear Moe repeat her mottoes. It made her sound and feel cheap. Like she was a teenage hooker or prostitute selling herself to the highest bidder? Was that the reality of her existence? Was it true and she wondered how a man who sees her like a whore could want to be with her. Keyla felt the tears building up inside of her. For the first time she was ashamed of who and how she was as a person. She started to run away, but Moe grabbed her arm and turned her toward him.

(Moe)"Keyla, all that I'm saying is that I don't think that how you act represents who you truly are inside.

(Keyla)" How do you know? Maybe all I am is a slut and a hoe that niggas can pay for. The price ain't even that high. Maybe that's who I be, who I am."

(Moe)"No Keyla, maybe you're that sweet little girl who deserves happiness. Maybe you're that woman whose innocence was robbed from her and taken away. Maybe you're that woman who's been told so often to use sex as a tool: that you do. Maybe you just have to ask yourself what it is you need sometimes instead of what you want."

(Keyla)"Maybe we should change the subject?" Keyla said with glassy eyes.

(Moe)" Fine. In fact do me a favor."

(Keyla)" What?"

(Moe)"Walk from here to there for me please."

Key turns around and walks like he asked her to and then returns to him. Moe shakes his head and gives applause.

(Keyla)"What was that all about?" Keyla said curiously.

(Moe)"I just wanted to see you walk. Ever since I've known you Key, I've loved watching you walk. Besides, since I upset you, it's only fair that an honest compliment come next."

She was dumbfounded. She had had no idea that Moe watched her walk. Keyla was overwhelmed and so happy that his compliment wasn't vulgar. Eventhough she was aware that the compliment meant that he liked her ass, she appreciated the fact that he dressed it up.

(Keyla)"So, you like my ass Moe?"

Without hesitation, Moe responds.

(Moe)"Actually, everything that you have is lovely and you move it very well. In fact, in that little silver dress that you are wearing, you look like one of those stars up there. You walked right out of the sky and brightened up my night. You walk just like a dream. Thanks Key. And again, I apologize if I insulted you in anyway, because it was not my intention."

The young woman had no words. Nothing that she knew how to say could express what she felt at that very moment. Keyla looked into Moe's eyes and was afraid, very afraid. Because he now had power over her, even if he didn't realize it, it was there none the less. He asked her if she was all right and if something was wrong. Keyla said no and put her head on his chest. Then with a tear in her eye she looked up at him, while her expression begged for him to kiss her lips. Moe smiled at her and gazed longingly in her eyes, but did not give her a kiss.

(Moe)"Keyla, it would be wrong of me to kiss you, while you're feeling so vulnerable. It might just confuse you further."

(Keyla)"You just don't want to. You don't want to kiss a piece of pretty trash, which can't compare to your miss perfect. I bet if I was Stephanie, you'd be tonguing me down instead of apologizing. Get off of me and leave me alone!"

Keyla runs away and leaves Moe standing there dazed and shocked by the events. He watched her leave and followed from a safe distance, making sure that she got home ok, All of the while, he thought to himself that she walked so well.

Steph and Slide argue about Moe

(Slide)"Yo, Steph! Stephanie! Who dat muthafucka you always talking to. That tall cat that's always up in yo grill, what's that nigga name?"

(Steph)"Why are you yelling at me?"

(Slide)"You better watch your mouth girl and answer my damn question. What's that muthafucka's name?"

(Steph)"That's not a muthafucka, that's my friend. His name is Moe. He's my best friend as a matter of fact. If you must know?" She says defiantly.

(Slide)"Fuck that shit. Now that I'm your man, you can't be havin' no best friends that's no niggas. I ain't havin that shit. So cut the bullshit and tell brotha man to step the fuck off. And do that shit fast." He says with a matter of fact tone.

Stephanie hesitates in disbelief and looks bewilderedly at her girlfriends. She could not believe that Slide was screaming at her in front of her friends and trying to make her give up Moe. He had crossed the line and she was going to let him know exactly how she felt.

(Steph)"Boy, you better check yourself and kill that noise. Moe is my best Goddamned friend and I'm not gonna stop talking to him. I ain't yo child and you ain't my daddy. So you can kill that nonsense and stop showing off for your boys. Cause I am not having it." She said as she waved her hand at him and shook her head with much attitude.

(Slide)"Oh ah'ight, so you telling me no?"

(His boys)"You gonna let her do you like that over some other nigga? You better put her in her place."

(Key and Cherry)"What the fuck you mean, put my girl in her place. Her place is in the sun, shinning on punk niggas like y'all. Y'all niggas is buggin hard and need to bounce with all of the bullshit!"

(Steph)"Yeah. We can talk about this later in private."

But before Stephanie could finish her thought, Slide slapped her as hard as he could. She fell to the ground and then he jumped on top of her still swinging. She started to cry and scream. Keyla jumped on Slide's back and started to pull at his hair. He threw her off of his back and his friends held her back. She kicked and yelled, but couldn't get away. While she did that, Cherry ran to get Moe.

(Slide)"Bitch. How dare you tell me no." He slaps at her face again, but hits her shoulder.

"Who the fuck you think you are? I will beat yo ass and teach you some respect. Shit I ain't yo daddy, but I'll beat yo ass like I am."

Just as he was about to punch her in her stomach, Moe ran up behind him and grabbed his arm.

(Moe)"What the fuck is wrong wit you nigga. Beating on a woman like that. Try that shit with me, wit ya punk ass. I'll beat ya faggot ass."

Slide swung up at Moe, who stood about six or seven inches taller than him, but missed. After that, Moe grabbed him and punched him in the jaw, knocking him against the wall. Then he snatched him up by his collar and threw him over a bench. Slide's friends rushed Moe and tried to grab and hold him down. They were unsuccessful, since Moe was too big for them to contend with. Besides that, Moe's two older brothers had come outside to see what all of the commotion was about. As a result Slide would have to fight him alone or leave. He stood up, brushed himself off and told Stephanie to come with him.

(Slide)" Stephanie. It's either him or me. I'm sorry that I hit you baby, but I was jealous. You always talkin' to or about that nigga, so I got mad. But I'm really sorry baby and I love you. Let's just go to my spot and make up. Please. Get the baby and let's be out, o.k."

Slide was so good at reading Stephanie. He

knew that if he mentioned the child and feigned interest in their being a family-like entity, she'd break down and come with him. Moe knew what Slide was doing and hoped that Stephanie did too. He prayed that the violence would wake her up to the reality of her situation. Moe wished that the fight would show her who really loved her. He would be greatly disappointed by his friend on that day. It broke his heart and shook his resolve when Stephanie brushed herself off, picked up her child and left with the pretty man. The same one who had just tried to beat her senseless, because she embarrassed him in front of his friends.

Moe left the scene dejected and appalled by the actions of his friend. He was so stunned that his body felt like it was going numb. He knew what it all meant and it made him cry. He knew at that very moment, that Steph was in deep trouble and that he would have to watch her suffer. The woman that he loved was now under the control of a violent man whom she believes loves her. Stephanie had to be saved from Slide and from herself. However, he had no clue of where to start or of what to do. All that he knew for sure was that life had put a really bitter taste in his mouth and left a thorn in his heart.

Two days after his fight with Slide, Moe sat in front of his building and waited to speak with Stephanie. He waited two hours before she showed up, then cautiously approached her on the stairwell and asked about what had happened the other day.

(Moe)'' Steph. Talk to me. Tell me how you could stay in a relationship with someone like him."

(Steph)" Moe, stop it. Do not talk about my man. I know he ain't perfect, but he is still my man. Plus he loves me. He tells me all of the time and I can tell that it's true."

Even though, deep down inside she wasn't as sure as she sounded. But Slide was a good thing. Wasn't he a good thing? Stephanie couldn't really make up her mind about Slide, but she liked the status that the relationship brought with it.

(Moe)" Stephanie. You honestly believe that a man you've known for less than a month really loves you?"

(Steph)" What? You've never heard of love at first sight?" She said this facetiously; knowing that Moe has always loved her. Shit. He's probably loved her since the first time his eyes saw her face. He sensed her sarcasm and responded in kind.

(Moe)" O.K. But, umm, how do you see love through a black eye? Isn't it kind of blurry with a bruised cornea?"

(Steph)" You are so fucked up. That was uncalled for. I got this bruised face defending our friendship. Sticking up for our connection. He got jealous, so he reacted. It's as much your fault as it is his."

(Moe)" What? Did you hear yourself say that just now? So, I made the man who loves you, beat you up in public, in front of your friends and your daughter? I told him to disrespect you and do something that no man should ever do: hit a woman. No, that's bullshit. He took your self respect all by himself and you let him."

(Steph)" Whatever, Moe. I'm not trying to hear you right now." And before she could catch herself, something terrible came out of her mouth. One of the worse things that she could have possibly said. "You just mad that he fucking me every day and you not."

He just looked at her in awe. Then he turned quickly and walked away. Crushed. His biggest dream deferred until another day, or just gone. Even after all of the harsh words, Moe knew that he would always love Stephanie. However, at that moment he refused to love her more than she loved herself.

Stephanie cried after Moe walked away. She knew that her words could not be taken back. She saw the pain in his eyes. She'd probably thrown the best thing in her life away and couldn't figure out why. Why did she choose the pretty violent man over the cute, respectful and reliable one? She desperately hoped that her best friend would still be her best friend after what was said. She kept her fingers crossed.

Moe walked aimlessly for what seemed like hours. His thoughts were jumbled and kept running into each other. He just couldn't conceive it or make it make sense. How could his best friend, the woman of his dreams, stay with an obsessive and abusive man? And on top of that, how could she throw his love back in his face as if it were a dirty rag or something? She knew that he loved her with all of his heart and she couldn't care less. It was painfully clear to him that she'd rather dodge Slide's 'loving' fist of fury, than run to his open arms. He could see it clearly now, but would probably never understand.

All of sudden, Moe found himself standing in front of Keyla's apartment, about to knock on the door. With a huge lump in his throat and sweat on his brow, he knocked. He didn't know why he was there or what would happen, but there he was.

Keyla heard the knock at her door, so she jumped out of the shower and wrapped herself in a towel. She opened the door dripping wet from head to toe. Moe looked at her with wide-eyed lust. Key was so shocked to see him at the door. But was even more surprised to see the way that Moe was looking at her wet, red towel covered body. She couldn't believe that he wanted her. But in a minute there would be no doubt in her mind about his desire. Every inch of her body would know for certain, exactly how much he wanted her.

(Key)" Hey Moe. What ya doing here?"

(Moe)" I'm not really sure, but I know that it's a better place than where I'm coming from. I wanted to come be with you."

(Key)" You don't want to be with me. Every body know that you love Stephanie. You always have and probably always will." Keyla said as she went to walk away. But Moe grabbed her and pulled her up against his chest. Her towel fell to the floor as he lifted her up off of the ground to kiss her. He put her down and gazed longingly at her form.

(Moe)" Key, you're right. I love Stephanie, but that doesn't matter so much anymore. She doesn't appreciate me, so I'm going to stop following her around like a sick puppy. Besides, the only thing on my mind right now, is putting a pretty piece of caramel in my mouth."

Before she could say anything, Moe grabbed her by the hand and led her to the couch. He whispered for her to close her eyes. Then with his fingertips, he slowly traced a path from her soft pouting lips down through the center of her ample breasts. Her chest heaved and her body shook ever so slightly, as his mouth touched her neck at the same time that his fingers slid lightly across her nipples. Keyla's nipples swelled as the blood quickly rushed into them. Then without warning he lifted her up into the air and sat her ample bottom in the palms of his hands. Her legs began to quiver and she felt a little dizzy as Moe opened her legs in front of his face. She spread them nervously, but willingly. Her heart pounded faster as she felt his warm breath get closer to her love. The anticipation of his tongue touching her there was driving her crazy. She squirmed so much that she almost fell from her perch, however his strong fingers refused to let that happened. Moe steadied his treat and began slowly sampling it with his tongue.

He could smell her excitement and lost himself in her aroma. Keyla was incredible and he intended to enjoy every inch of her. He could hear the sound that her love made in response to his tongue circling her clitoris. It was the sweetest thing that Moe had heard in a long time and he hoped to hear it often. The young woman shook almost violently. It was like his mouth had opened a dam. Keyla climaxed so hard that her pussy released a thick flow of her excitement. Moe eagerly cleaned up the mess that he had made.

(Key)" Damn".

She wanted Moe so badly now. So she stood up immediately reaching for and finding his manhood. It was impressive and she was glad. Keyla unzipped his pants and pulled him out of his confinement. She squeezed his throbbing tool and jerked it vigorously. His eyes rolled back into his head, while the young lady jerked him off. The tip of his dick was swollen and throbbing. He was so anxious.

(Key)" Close your eyes and relax. Let me taste you now, umm."

She purred like a cat and pulled his pants all of the way off. Then she blew her warm breath along the inside of his thigh until she reached the base of his penis. Without warning, she opened her mouth wide and lowered her head down on to him. Her tongue made a trail from the head of his cock down in between his testicles. She now had what appeared to be 8 inches of man tickling the back of her throat. He was amazed at her ability to take his pride and joy with such pleasurable ease. It was the first time that Moe had felt the back of a woman's orifice squeezing the tip of him. He was literally blown away.

Keyla treated him like he was the best thing that her mouth had ever encountered. She licked, squeezed, stroked, pulled, and sucked on his dick for what seemed like an eternity. Moe squirmed and held his breath so that his mountain wouldn't erupt before he had learned what it was like to have Keyla wrapped around him in every conceivable way.

(Moe)" Key. Take the condom out of my pocket and come here.

(Key)" You want my pussy, Moe? You want to fuck me now? Huh, is that what you want?"

(Moe)" Nah Key. I want you to make love to me, because I want to make love to you."

As a teardrop built up in the corner of her eye, she straddled his lap and looked deeply into his eyes. She was hooked. Moe would be the first man to make sincere passionate love to her and touch her deeply. She had had orgasms before that curled her toes, but this was the first time that a man had a tool big enough to touch her heart. With every deep penetrating stroke Moe was tearing her open. It was as if she was losing her virginity all over again: emotionally. She didn't know whether or not she loved the man, but she knew that she needed him. There was no doubt in her heart about that fact. Moe was a good guy, who was good for her and Keyla was happily afraid of what would happen next, but definitely willing to find out. The two loved like nothing else mattered. Like there bodies needed each other to survive and only the need to replenish energies could stop them.

The Morning after For Keyla and Moe

He watched the sun come up, through the window across the room and gazed at her sleeping face as a beam of light illuminated it. She really was a beautiful woman, is what Moe thought to himself. He had no regrets and no remorse. Not to mention no energy, since they had loved each other four times the night before. His body was spent, but the young man was too confused to sleep. How could he have made love to Keyla, when his heart belonged to Stephanie?

Moe was nervous and a little afraid. He didn't know what to expect or how to act. What would he say to those big brown eyes when they opened? What would she say? Was this a one night stand or could they make it into something more? Actually, he knew that it wasn't a one stand, at least not for him. And he hoped that it wasn't one for her either, because it felt too nice to be over once the sun came up. Something that felt that nice should last longer than a day. But Moe wondered if Key could go through with something more than just a sexual relationship between the two of them. After all, she knew where his heart was and maybe that would be just a little too much for her?

All of a sudden, Key opened her big brown eyes and began to smile, because Moe was still there. She'd thought that it was a dream, but it wasn't. It was very real. She had slept with Moe. : Stephanie's Moe. And he had turned her out. She was his to do with what ever he pleased and she hoped he'd be gentle, at least most of the time. This was all new territory for her. She was beginning to love a man for whom he was and how he made her feel, instead of loving what he had. Even though, after last night, she did love something that he had and wanted as much of it as possible.

(Key)" Mornin. I'm glad that you stayed. I was kinda scared you'd be gone when I woke up. Like a dream or something."

(Moe)" Nah, It wasn't a dream. It was very real. In fact, it was beautiful. I thoroughly enjoyed myself. Not to mention, every inch of you."

After he said this, he pulled back the covers and ran his fingers slowly over every inch of her body. He smiled and so did she.

(Moe)" My fingers had no idea that you looked so good. You are so attractive and just too sexy. Come here girl and let me hold you."

She moved closer to him and melted into his arms. Key rested her head on his chest and listened to his heartbeat. It was pounding almost as loudly as hers was pounding. It was so amazing to her. She could not believe that Moe was so into her.

(Key)" Moe is it over? Was one night enough for you?" She looked up at him with questioning eyes and held her breath waiting for his answer.

(Moe)" Key, I...,"

(Key)" No Moe, that's okay. Don't say anything. I don't want this to end just yet. So please don't say anything. Just hold me, okay."

Moe squeezed her tightly and kissed her forehead. He felt her trembling in his arms. It amazed him how a woman so tough, just a few days ago, could be so vulnerable and afraid today. He was confused, but he knew that he would not let his feelings for Steph make him hurt Key. He knew that he didn't love her and that he loved Stephanie, however last night was definitely more than just sex to him. It was special. It was sweet. And it was definitely worth doing again, as often as possible.

(Moe)"You have so much more to offer a man, than just your body. And if you don't mind, I'd like us to spend some real time together. Maybe we could do some things and go some places sometimes, just the two of us. That way I can experience you for who you really are, on a one to one basis. If you'd like to do that?"

(Key)" I'd like that. You can show me some of

that culture you're always talking about. Help me become the queen of the Nile or at least the queen of the hood."

(Moe)" As a matter of fact, we should get up, get dressed and go get some breakfast. I'd cook for you, but I don't want your mother to catch me here."
It was nice. Two people who needed each other had found each other. Keyla had found a man who would respect her and treat her like a lady, while Moe had found a woman who would love him if he'd let her. Things were about to get very interesting.

Break

He still couldn't believe it: the way that circumstances changed lives in an instant. It was mind boggling and beautiful all at once. He couldn't believe that he had slept with Keyla and at the same time, was glad that the smell of her was still on him. However, what really threw him was how much he enjoyed being with her. Not just physically either, but emotionally. The young man was completely surprised by the young lady from the ghetto. She was substantial, interesting and fun to be around. And he certainly wanted to be around her. However, before he could be with her, on any terms, there were some things that had to be taken care of. The biggest of which, was the fact that

Stephanie was the woman that he loved and Keyla was her best friend. Which one did he want most: the fantasy or the reality?

On the one hand there was Stephanie who he'd dreamed about ever since that first day some ten odd years ago. And on the other hand there was Keyla, who had recently caught him by surprise and made him warm inside. What would he do? How and who would he choose?

(Moe)" Damn. I am so very confused. I have definitely done it now. On the rebound from Stephanie, I've gone and slept with Keyla. And surprisingly enough, I don't regret it. I'm just baffled by the whole thing. The question is what to do now. Do I pursue a relationship with a woman who obviously wants me or do I hurt her feelings because of my desire for her friend? Wait a minute; let me think this through, as thoroughly as possible. First of all, I have no clue about how or what Stephanie feels for me, if anything at all. Secondly, Keyla's past is littered with promiscuity, so maybe I'm making too much of the whole thing. I could have just been another piece of ass to her. Nah, I don't really think that, but anything is possible. I wonder if she'll tell Steph what happened. If she'll tell Cherry? Or will she want to be with me in a committed relationship, even though I don't have big dough and I don't have a ride? If she's that shallow, I don't want to be with her anyway, but I hope she's not. What am I saying? Am I falling for Keyla too? I mean, I've always noticed her. But as a man, how could you not notice a woman as attractive as she is? So do I just want her for her body or could I feel for her what I've always felt for Stephanie?"

Stephanie interrupted his thoughts when she knocked on his apartment door.

(Steph)" Hey, Moe." She said in a whisper and waited for him to ask her in. She hoped that he would let her inside and not just shut the door in her face.

(Moe)" Hey, Steph. What brings you here? What can I do for you?"

His voice was stiff and almost cold. The sound of it cut her to the quick. She never expected him to ever talk to her like that. It startled her and it hurt. But deep down inside, she knew that it was her own fault. She knew that her words had caused the friction between them.

(Steph)" Moe. I just came to apologize and try to make things right between us again. This thing with you and me kept me up all night. I want us to make up and be friends again, if that's o.k., with you. Be the man that you've always been. The one who keeps me sane and takes care of me."

Her words were so sincere and heartfelt that they almost made him forget every thing that had happened. But He didn't forget any of it. How could he not remember watching the woman of his dreams get slapped down, hearing her denounce his love, or most of all, the way that Keyla smiled at him after they made love.

(Moe)" Steph, don't worry. We will always be friends, but the job of protecting you from yourself is vacant because I can't do it any more. Actually, I could, but it hurts too badly. So I won't. I think that I'll protect myself this time."

(Steph)" What? You're gonna let an argument end what we have. You're gonna let my yelling mean things, that I never meant to say ruin a connection that's lasted nearly ten years. Aren't we worth more than that to you? Don't you love me? Don't you Moe?"

(Moe)" Of course I love you. I have since the first day that we met. And you've always known this fact, but never cared enough to do any thing about it. But that's o.k. I'm sure that you have your reasons. However, I can't take it any more. I've had enough. Always having to watch someone else receive your affection. Always being the good secretly in love friend, who waited patiently for his chance, his opportunity to bask in the glow of your eyes. To know what it felt like to kiss the prettiest, softest looking lips that I'd ever seen part and pronounce my name. Hoping that secretly some where deep down inside of you there was a place for me. A spot where I'd be kept warm and could graciously return the favor."

(Steph)" Moe I never knew."

(Moe)" Steph, don't lie. It's ok. I don't hate you or anything like that; I'm just tired of being so close and not being able to love you, at least not openly or intimately.
So I'm revealing my feelings to you finally, in the hope of getting past them. So like I said, we'll always be friends but I need to find myself a healthy fulfilling relationship. By the way, I don't mean to be rude but I have an appointment and don't want to be late. So we should talk about this some other time."

He closed the door and ended the conversation. He'd finally done it: taken the biggest emotional step of his life. Moe had let his desire for Stephanie out of its hiding place and into the sun. Now the fantasy would have to exist in the real world. Would it dissolve easily into an obscure memory or stick around for awhile making things interesting?

Steph's Revelations

She sat in her room with her friend and cried for what seemed like hours, holding Joy and wondering why life was so hard on her. She couldn't figure out the events of the past few days. How could the pretty well to do man that she gave herself to, abuse her? And how could the one person who was reliable in her whole world give up on her?

(Steph)" Cherry. How could he say those things? How could he admit his love and give up on me in the same breath? It's not fair. It's just not fair."

(Cherry)" Stop crying girl. I know it hurts, but don't cry. Besides, you have Slide and he is the one that you want. Isn't he?"

(Steph)" I don't know what I want. But I do know that Moe means a lot more to me than some nigga with a fat dick and a fat ride does. The sad part is that until Moe decided to take his love away from me, I never knew how much I wanted it."

(Cherry)" You love that nigga. I can't believe it. How could you love him all of this time and not show him? That's fucked up Steph. That's some shit you do to no good niggas that don't deserve your heart, but not nice brothas like Moe."

(Steph)" I know. I know. But I thought there would always be time for us to be together. As long as he loved me, there'd always be time. Now I've lost the only real man that I've ever met. What am I supposed to do now?"

(Cherry)" Did you tell him that you love him too? Does he know all of this stuff you telling me? Does he?"

(Steph)" No."

(Cherry)" So go to him and tell him that you love him."

Stephanie ran back to Moe's apartment determined to tell him how she felt about him. She was going to confess her love and ask for forgiveness. She was so anxious and so nervous. The entire way there her mind wondered making up scenarios.

(Steph)" Maybe he'll cry when I tell him? After all he is a sensitive brother. Or maybe he'll snatch me up in his arms and kiss me passionately? I've always wanted to kiss those full lips of his. No, umm, maybe he'll say nothing and then just take me by the hand lead me inside of the house? Finally, having the opportunity to release all of his built up passion for me. I can't even imagine what that would feel like, but I'm gonna find out. I'm gonna find out today, one way or another. If after I've opened up my heart to him, if the man still hesitates, I'm gonna jump his bones and take advantage of him. Then we'll tell the world how we........"

She was stopped in mid thought by a sight that was unimaginable. It was something that she would have never guessed or believed, not even in her wildest dreams. There they were Moe and Keyla, two of her dearest friends, kissing each other in front of his door. It was horrible. They were standing there touching each other's bodies and acting like lovers. Her Moe was touching Key like he couldn't get enough of her. Like he wanted her. No, it was even worse than that. It was like he needed her. It made her feel sick.

Stephanie's heart was beating louder than anything that she had ever heard before in her whole life. It was deafening. She didn't even notice that there were tears flowing from her eyes. Her body began to hurt. She felt hot and angry all at once. Both broken and betrayed. She wondered why Keyla was where she wanted to be and how she got there. Moe was supposed to be hers and hers alone, not Keyla's.

(Steph)."What the hell is this?"
The two lovebirds turned simultaneously and looked at the distraught young woman: their friend.

(Steph)" How could you? Keyla, how could

you do this to me? You're supposed to be my girl. One of my oldest friends."

(Key)" Hold up Steph. I didn't do anything to you. All I did was something for me. I noticed that a nice guy liked me and I took full advantage of my luck, instead of playing games with his affection and treating him all messed up and shit."

(Moe)" Chill, Key. There's no need for that. You don't have to be so mean about it."

(Key)"Oh, so you still defend her. You gonna fuck me, but protect her. What the fuck is that all about."

(Steph)"What? You fucked her. You needed pussy that bad that you fucked Key? Shit. How much did you pay for it?"

Stephanie didn't mean any of the things that came out of her mouth, but she was angry and hurt. So she lashed out at the people who had made her hurt. She needed them to share her pain and wanted them to feel some kind of guilt for their connection.
(Key)[With tear filled eyes]

"Yeah. I fucked him. No, as a matter of fact, I made mad passionate love to him. It was beautiful, sweet and absolutely free, you slow missing out on good dick, bitch. And he can have as much of this pussy that his big dick, having heart desires. As a matter of fact, this man can have all of me, so he don't fucking need no chick that knows that he loves her and don't give a fuck. Because I give a fuck, so fuck you."

(Steph) "You're right Key. I did do him wrong. And I'm sorry for that. I am so very, very sorry Moe. It's true. I knew that you loved me, but just wasn't mature enough to do what I needed to. The idea of getting into a relationship with a real man, at such an early age was just a little too intimidating. I should have told you. What's that you always tell me, hindsight is 20/20', now I know what you mean. I can see how open your heart was

to me, now that it's too late. I wish that it wasn't. I should have told you a long time ago that I love you so much, but I didn't. And now I'm sorry."

The young lady ran off crying her heart out and kicking herself emotionally, for being such a fool. She wondered what she would do now. Her thoughts were jumbled and unclear, so she ran as fast as she could, away from it all. Maybe if she ran fast enough and far enough, it would change something? Maybe if she ran hard enough and held her breath long enough, the pain and confusion would get left behind? Stephanie had just found her love for Moe, but because of her bad timing, was losing herself. She had set her love for him free and couldn't take it back. The young lady hoped that he'd embrace her and her feelings and then show her what to do. Teach her how to use it. How to let her love lead her to happiness. But he belonged to someone else now, so she would have to find her own way. Stephanie kept on running.

Break

Keyla grabbed Moe's arm and held him tightly. Yelling at him and pulling with all of her might, attempting to stop him from doing what he's always done: run after Stephanie.

(Key)" Moe don't go after her! Leave her alone. Don't be her little puppy dog that always runs after her and licks her feet after sniffing her ass. Be a man! Be my man. Please. Do not go after Steph."

(Moe)" Key. How can I not go after her? She's my best friend and she's hurting right now. And it's all my fault. I have to do something. I need to make sure that she's ok. I'm her friend and that's what friends do. They take care of each other, when times are at their worse. They don't take the easy way out. They take the hard road with you, at your side or behind you and help you through it all."

(Key)" Whatever Moe. You just want to run after the woman of your dreams. The woman that you been sweatin' ya whole adult life, who just told you that she loves you. That's all you want. You want her. Fuck me! I'm just an easy piece of ass. Keyla couldn't possibly be girl or wife material."

(Moe)" How could you say that to me after what we've shared?"

(Key)" How could you do this to me?"

(Moe)" Key. You couldn't be more wrong. You are so much more than just ass to me. You are a breath of fresh air. But even still I have to go see if Stephanie is all right. She's my dearest friend and you should understand this."

(Key)" Yeah. And like I've heard you say so many times, she's the most important woman in your life, besides your momma. And who am I to stand in the way of that. Let true mother fucking love shine and take center stage, while passing interest exits stage left. Bye Moe. Go and get your girl."

Keyla stormed off leaving Moe with a choice of either chase the woman of your dreams who has a man and who has blown you off on numerous occasions, or go after an angry woman who has touched you intimately and put herself in your hands.

When Moe caught up with Stephanie, she was a basket case breathing irregularly and crying profusely. She was beyond distraught. She was a mess. A very beautiful mess. He could see her from a distance, sitting on the last step of the stoop. She glowed. Her body shimmered in the radiance of her guilt. It had strangely liberated her. She just seemed so different to him now. It was probably the fact that her love for him was now visible to the naked eye. Out in the open for everyone to see. Deep down inside he almost hated her. Almost. And he definitely couldn't understand her.

(Moe)" Steph. Stop crying. Talk to me. Let's work this thing out. Come here and tell me something. Is it true? Do you really love me?"

This was it. This was their moment of truth, when they would either put up or shut up. The time had come for them to place all of their feelings on the table.

(Steph)" Moe, I'm so sorry. Please believe me. I never ever wanted us to be like this. On opposite sides of each other feeling lost and confused. I just always wanted us to be the best of friends."

(Moe)" Never anything more? You never once thought about me being your man, before today? Did you? Please don't lie to me either Steph."

(Steph)" Honestly, no, never in a serious way. I mean, I had what if thoughts, but never any actual let me be with Moe thoughts. You aren't what I'm used to at all. You've always been a little too different for me."

(Moe)" Yeah, too broke, too average looking and too much of a nice guy."

(Steph)" Moe, you are all of those things, but you're also too much man for a girl like me. What could a woman who barely knows herself, do for a man who is so sure of himself? You take care of everything and everyone, including me. All I take care of is Joy and men who don't really know or care about me."

(Moe)" But how does that help me? How should I feel about it all? I only do what I do, because I care about my friends and family. I am who I am because of what they give back to me in return: genuine feelings of concern and love. So, help me be better. Tell me that you love me. If you love me, then tell me that you do."

(Steph)" Moe. I do love you."

(Moe)" But you're not in love with me. Or you really don't know how you feel. Am I close? Am I anywhere near the truth? Or maybe it's just too hard for you to love a man, who can't give you any status or luxury? Yeah, I don't fit that description. Shit. All that I can give a woman is unconditional love, respect, understanding and support. All of which doesn't add up to much in terms of dollars and cents. I'm just a broke ass nigga, who feels shit."

(Steph)" Moe stop it. It's not like that. That ain't it at all."

(Moe)" Okay. If it's not that, then why did you pick a drug dealer over me? And when he beat you up and robbed you of your self-respect, you still chose him over me. Why?

I need to understand this whole thing, so that my picture of us is clear and my life can go on.

His nerves were on edge, his stomach was one huge knot, his eyes were glassy and he had never felt anticipation this intense before in his life. Actually, that's not completely true. The first time that his lips touched Keyla's felt similar to this, but that was another circumstance to be dealt with another time. Right now, he needed to know why she never picked him and why the pretty woman never let him indulge in her delights. So he demanded an answer.

(Moe)" Steph, answer me. Tell me something. Please help me understand it all, because it's tearing me apart emotionally. I don't know how much more I can take."

(Steph)" Moe. You are the kind of guy that every young girl dreams about. The kind that any woman would be lucky to have. I mean, you do everything well and you're always putting others first. Shit, you're probably the only reason why I'm not crazy. You've always been my strength. And the minute that you said you were giving up on me, it all changed for me. I watched you walk away and my heart felt like it was breaking. At that moment, I knew that you were more than just my best friend: you were the best thing for me and the nicest thing in my life, other than Joy. I can't fully explain all of my choices and actions to you, hell I don't really understand them all myself. But this I do know: that I am in love with you and you are in love with me. It would be wrong of us not to explore something that feels so much bigger than the both of us."

(Moe)" What about Slide? When you see his pretty face, fancy car and remember how much money he has, what then? Will you still choose me and will I still be your man, if we take that step? Do you love him, or just what he has to offer?"

(Steph)" I was infatuated with him. The good looks, the money and the status, all struck a nerve with me. He represented everything that me and my girls always talked about, so of course I wanted him. Even when I saw that he was far from what I needed, I still wanted the status. Moe, don't you understand that every young woman born and raised in the projects wants to live ghetto fabulous at some point? To have status among her peers. So instead of looking for the educated nice guy with real potential, we seek out the ghetto superstars."

(Moe)"Okay, I get it. So why the change of heart all of a sudden? Actually, don't answer that. I already know the answer. You only want me now, because you saw me with Keyla."

(Steph)"That's not true. I've always wanted you in my life."

(Moe)"Yeah, that may be true. However, you've only decided to make me your man, because your girl and I slept together. You'd rather see me alone pining over you, than involved with someone and maybe even happy. It is so messed up, that you could be so fucking selfish, for so damn long. All of these years I've loved you unconditionally and whole-heartedly and watched you give yourself to others. So tell me why I should ruin what I've found with Keyla."

(Steph)"You're so wrong Moe. It was the thought of you leaving me that did it. Why do you think I was there in the first place? I was crying before I got there. Before I saw you kissing my girl. Talking to Cherry earlier helped me come to my senses about what I really wanted: I want you. Right here, right now, and for as long as possible. I know that I've probably broken your heart more than once, but please don't do it to me. Don't pick Key over me. Don't let some good sex cloud your judgement. Do what you've always told me to do: Weigh your options and decide what's best for you over the long term. Don't make a snap decision. Please. Please. Give me what you've always wanted me to give you: a chance."

(Moe)"I don't know, Steph. I just don't know."

An upset Key runs into Cherry

(Cherry)" Hey girl. What's the matter with you? Why you cryin girl? Shit. It must be bad, because I've never seen you cry. C'mon girl, tell your girl what happened."

(Key)"I'm alright. I just finished fighting with Steph and yelling at Moe."

(Cherry)"Why you fighting wit our girl? What she do to you. Kill your cat or something?"

(Key)"Naw, she stole my man."

(Cherry)"what the fuck you talking about? You ain't got no man. Besides, why would she want your imaginary man, when I just convinced her to tell Moe that she loves him?"

Suddenly Cherry stopped mid thought, dumbfounded by what crossed her mind. It could not be possible. Keyla couldn't possibly be standing in her face telling her that Stephanie's Moe was her man. But the never before seen tears, in Keyla's eyes were a clear indication that that was exactly what was being said.

(Cherry)"Key. You telling me, that you're fucking with Moe?"

(Key)" I'm not fucking with him. We made love last night for the first time and it blew me away.

He was gentle, he was strong and he was there when I woke up."

(Cherry)" You fucked Moe. Was it big? Did you cum? Can he fuck?"

(Key)" He fucked me all night long and kept me cumming, if you must know. But the bad shit is he touched me somewhere other than my spot. He turned my curiosity for him into lust and desire. He got me feeling shit that no nigga ever has. Stuff I didn't think any man could make me feel."

(Cherry)"That's deep as hell. Shit, that's beautiful, but you're fucked up. How could you go after Moe? You know that nigga off limits.

(Key) "He ain't got no girl, so why can't I have him?"

(Cherry)"Shit, you know him and Steph got that unspoken love thing going on. You know he got it bad for her and always has. Plus, she loves him. So for you to fuck wit him is foul. You broke the rule."

(Key)"I know. But I couldn't help it. He's the only real man that I've ever met and he noticed me. Shit he wanted me. Cherry, he wanted me, even knowing how I've been. It didn't matter to him. So I gave into it and I'm glad that I did. It was the best I ever had and I want more. No. I need more. I need him."

(Cherry)" Damn. This is some serious shit. Both my girls feeling the same nigga. Yo, the shit is about to hit the fan, because only one of you can have him."

(Key)" He picked her already. He's chasing after her right now. Then he's gonna make love to her and forget all about me and our night together. I never had a chance. No woman can compete with a man's childhood fantasy. Shit. To be with her, would be his dream come true. The sad part is that he's my dream."

Cherry held her friend and tried her best to comfort her, because she knew she was right. Stephanie had always been Moe's dream girl. Everyone in the neighborhood, who ever saw the two of them together, could tell that. He always looked at her like the sun rose and set in her eyes. Now she loved him too, so it's like his dream had finally come true. She was glad for Moe, because he's a good guy and deserves to be happy. But at the same time, she was sad for her girl Keyla, because the first time that her heart opened to a man should have been better. The man should have been available and willing to be with her, not in love with her best friend.

Moe Comes Back

(Moe)"Keyla, what's the matter?"

(Cherry)" That's a foolish question."

(Moe)" I don't think that I've ever seen you cry, in all the time that I've known you. And now you're crying because of me?"

(Key)" I'm not crying over you. I'm crying because I feel stupid. This love shit is over-rated and fucked-up. I was dumb enough to sleep wit you, knowing you digging my girl, so now I gotta deal wit it."

(Moe)" What are u talking about? I only ran after Stephanie, so that everything could be laid on the table. I did not run after her in order to make her my girl."
(Key)" You didn't?"
(Moe)" No. Hell, what kind of man did you think I was?"

(Key)" I don't know? I just know you've always loved her. So when you ran after her, it was easy to figure out why."

(Moe)" Well, I hate to disappoint you, but there is no way in hell that I could sleep with you last night and then go after your girl. I'd like to think that I'm a better man than that. Besides, how could I pick her, when for the past few days, you've been the only thing on my mind. Even before that first kiss, that drove me crazy. As a matter of fact pretty woman..."

He walked close to her, put his finger beneath her chin and raised her head. Her tear filled eyes met his and then she began to speak. He shushed her with his finger, wiped her tears away and kissed her deeply. Cherry was stunned. The pretty promiscuous woman could not believe her eyes. Stephanie's Moe had rejected her last minute love, for the opportunity to be with Keyla. It was astonishing.

(Moe)"Key. I'm sorry that I made you cry. But I tell you what, lets make those the last sad tears that I ever cause you. I don't make promises, but I will make every effort to keep what ever this is as interesting as possible. All you have to do is take my hand and let me take you where you need to go. Where ever that is."

(Key): But what about your love for Steph? How does that fit into all of this?"

(Moe)" It doesn't. I've realized that some loves are simply intangible. See, I've felt what I feel for your girl for so long, but never had the opportunity to share it with her. Because of that it could never be real. It's all just a dream that a young unrealistic man held onto for far too long."

(Key)" You sure. I don't want it to come back and haunt us. You know, just when I get comfortable it rears its head and bites me in the butt. I don't want that."

(Moe)" Think about it like this Key. My love for her was like a string of pearls. Priceless to me because it was love and deeply heartfelt. But you know how they say that pearls must be worn often and kept close to you or else they lose their luster. She ignored the love that I had for her, so it dulled."

(Cherry)" Damn, Moe. You are a really deep brother. Shit, I never thought about love like that before. You got some serious shit wit you."

(Key)" Yes he does. My man got some serious shit with him."

Key smiled, put her hand in his and then they walked side by side toward their apartment building.

CHAPTER 2

The bathroom was filled with candlelight that danced romantically around the room. Candles that smelled like peaches surrounded the tub and there was a hint of vanilla in the air. The water was warm and filled with bubbles, when he stepped into it and then sat her down in between his legs. He bathed her slowly with tender fingers that lingered at every curve. He allowed his fingers to indulge themselves with the feel of her flesh. They loved the nape of her neck and the rise of her breast. For Moe, there were very few things that came close to the feel of her mammary glands in the palms of his hands.

He stood her up, wrapped her in a towel and then carried her to his bed. Gently he laid her down and then reached for the oil. The massage that followed was Keyla's favorite part of their foreplay, because it relaxed her and made her ready for him. Afterward, she lay there while he retrieved a bowl from the freezer. When Moe returned Keyla was lying at the foot of the bed with her legs up and spread eagle. The silk handkerchief that he had asked her to put on covered her eyes. The anticipation had her as wet as she'd ever been. He could see the moist droplets on the hair surrounding her pouty lips.

She could feel the chill coming from the bowl as he sat it in between her eagerly parted legs. Moe took a rather large strawberry from the bowl and put it next to her lips, barely touching them. Her body shook as he slowly inserted it into her pretty pussy. She moaned and shivered slightly. He could hear the sound of her moisture as it engulfed the berry. Then he licked around the edge of her love, caressing the tip of her clit, with his tongue. Then his tongue entered her searching for the strawberry. The fruit rolled back onto his tongue covered with her thick cream. She cooed as he chewed and crunched on the flesh of the cum covered piece of fruit. It was delicious.

(Moe)" Keyla. Baby. Strawberries taste so much better with cream on them."

He dipped another in her love box and stuck it half way in his mouth. Then he put his mouth to hers so that she could taste for herself.

(Moe)" Umm, how's that love? Isn't that the sweetest thing you've ever tasted?"

(Key)"Huh, umm (Crunch). Yes. My pussy tastes so good on your lips.

Then the young man broke a frozen banana in half, as he flipped her over onto her knees. He gazed longingly at the lovely sight, while putting the frozen banana half in his mouth. Next he traced the side of her gash with the ice-cold tip of the fruit, before sliding it deep inside of her. Her muscle squeezed and began to melt the fruit. Moe's mouth fucked her with the freezing yellow tool. Keyla went crazy. She'd never helped a man make a banana pudding that way before. It was messy, tasty and fun, especially the way that Moe licked her bowl and cleaned up his mess hungrily.

There was always something exotic and sensual about their lovemaking. It always began slowly and never seemed to want to come to an end. Keyla wasn't sure if she loved the man, but his dick would have a place in her heart for a long time. Not to mention a place in her mouth, in her pussy and even in her tight fat ass that he loved so much.

Steph in Shock

"Stephanie thought to herself while she walked home after her encounter with Moe."

(Steph)"What the hell happened? How could the man, who has always loved me, not choose to be with me? It makes no sense at all. I mean, who walks away from the opportunity that they claim they've always wanted? Without even looking back? Damn Key and Moe are going to be a couple. Lovers. He's gonna take care of her now and give her all of his attention. She won't let him share his time with me, knowing that I love him. Even though he says that he'll still be there for me and probably will, it won't be the same. I feel like two of my best friends just cut my throat. They're probably somewhere right now fucking. Or worse than that, they are probably somewhere falling in love. I'll miss him. I'll miss the person that I am because of him."

A broken and dejected Steph headed home shouting at herself in her mind. She began to not like herself just a little. It was almost as if losing Moe had put the tiniest hole in her spirit and she could feel herself slipping through it. The slow drip of self-dissolution.

She wondered who she'd be without him in her face all the time pointing out the right things to do. Would the affects that Moe had had on her for so long, wear off, as distance grew and time passed?

(Steph)"How could he do this to me? He's supposed to always be there. Like he always used to say,'ever present'. I know what that means, now that he's gone. But it's my own fault."

Stephanie bumps into Cherry and her mother, while walking around in her depressed state.

(Cherry)"Hey girl. You o.k. You look a little out of it. What's the matter"? She asked partially knowing the answer before hand.

(Steph)"What...umm. Hey. What did you say?" She answered in a confused tone.

(Ms. James)"She asked you, what was the matter and why you look so lost girl. That's what she said."

Cherry's mother Ms. Lorna Louise James is sassy with an edge of sarcasm attached to it. She's 37 years old and had Cherry when she was 17. The woman has been divorced twice, but of course swears that she knows everything about love. In essence, she's bitter, loud and tactless with an opinion on everything.

(Steph)"I'm just a little tired. I just need some rest."

(Cherry)"You sure you don't want to talk? I'm

here for you, girl."

(Steph)"No. I'm all right. I'm just gonna go to the house and try to relax.

(Lorna)"Child it's alright. We know ya hurting. We know Moe done hooked up with Keyla. The damn boy shocked us all. Shit. I know it shocked me. 'Cause I thought yous two was involved and foolin around. Hell the boy was always up under you. I thought you had done put it on him."

(Cherry)"Ma, cut it out."

(Lorna)"I'm just sayin what I know and what I thought I saw. And I'm yo mamma, so don't be shushing me. I ain't tryin to hurt the girl any more than she already is. I likes the girl."

Steph stood there in disbelief. Not believing that Cherry's mother already knew that Moe had rejected her for Keyla. And she knew that if Ms. James knew, soon everyone would know. Since she acted like it was her patriotic, civic and neighborly duty to tell everyone's business to everybody.

(Lorna)"It's just a shame that she led the boy on and now he sleeping with her friend. It's like I always say, if you don't give a man what he want, hell what he need, some other woman will."

(Steph)"Thanks for the information, that I'm sure I didn't already know Ms. James."

Stephanie rolled her tear filled eyes and then stormed off. Leaving her friend and her friend's insensitive, overbearing mother to undoubtedly discuss her plight. As if it didn't hurt badly enough, now she'll be the laughing stock of the projects. She would be avoiding the public eye for a long time. It hurt badly enough without their judgmental scrutiny. She'd be a pretty hermit for a while, at least until they found something else to talk about.

Break

(Cherry)"Momma, why you always got to do dat. Get all up in my friend's business and stuff. Giving advice when nobody asked for none."

(Lorna)"Cause I'm a adult and I done been down that road that they going down. So I just want to pass on some of my wisdom and knowledge to love and things. That's why. And I done told you to watch ya mouth young lady. Talking to me like I'm one of your snot nosed, hot assed friends. Don't forget I'm ya mamma. You hear me?"

(Cherry)"I know Momma. But why you always gotta be like that? That's why my friends don't come over that much. And after you put my girl Steph's feeling out on display like that, I'm sure she won't be visiting me any time soon."

(Lorna)"Now I already done told you that I wasn't trying to hurt the child feelings. And besides, you know I'm right anyway. Tell me what I said ain't true."

(Cherry)"Yeah, you right. Cause if I wasn't her girl and didn't have the 411 from the inside, I'd swear that Moe and Steph was fucking too. Oops. Sorry 'bout that mamma. But that is true. Moe be following her around like she couchie whipped him and he don't know what to do."

(Lorna)"See that. I told you I was not trying to be mean or nosy. I was just saying the truth out loud. But I'm still trying to figure the other girl out though. That Keyla girl, usually only pays attention to the fancy brothers. So what she see in that smart, broke behind Morece? I can't put my finger on that one."

(Cherry)"Yup. That one got me at first too ma. But then I talked to her about it. That nigga Moe and all that sweet talk got her thinking he the best thing in the world. She was so emotional and shook up when we was talking. She sounded like she love that man. He done put some good loving on her ass."

(Lorna)"Shit. You got to watch them quiet men with them sweet words. Them the ones that talk to you soft and sweet while they dick talking to you hard and long. That shit put together is some powerful mojo. Get you feeling so good, you don't know if you are coming or going? That was like your daddy girl. He was an average looking (sweet-talking) nice guy who could suga talk you right out of your panties. Have you sharing Vicky Secret on the first date. Damn! His stuff was so good; it could make you lose time. That's what's going on with your girlfriend Keyla. She done fell in love with the loving."

Break

Part 2

Most people don't realize it, but time passes you by faster than the wind does. You feel it surround you and catch you up in its moment, but you never really notice when it changes. You know that it is different, maybe a little cooler? But you can't recall when it changed. Time does that same thing to people. It lets you know that you are living in a particular instant and then it's gone. That time frame that you were just in is suddenly just a memory never to be had again.

Stephanie understands this all too well. Her moment with Moe had come and gone and was now only a reflection. One that she wishes was less clear sometimes, because then maybe it wouldn't hurt so badly when she opened her eyes. She wished that he were still close enough to hold on to and near enough to squeeze, when her pillow wasn't enough. She missed him like heaven does the rain the morning after the thunderstorm. But what could she do? She blew her opportunity and, in her mind, probably her one true shot at happiness. So for a while the young lady would beat herself up and also stay close enough to Slide for him to offer his assistance.

(Slide)"Steph hurry your lazy ass up. And finish putting that shit in them bags. And don't be wasting none of it either". An always, angry Slide yells out to his battered and bruised, live in sweetheart.

(Steph)"You better watch your mouth girl. Before I come back there and fix it for you."

Stephanie froze up and raised her eyes to the mirror in front of her. She touched her seemingly always, bruised right cheek and stared at herself for a moment. And as always, her pride hurt her more than any punch or (over aggressive fuck session) could.

Suddenly, he grabbed her by the back of her head and pushed her face against the clouded mirror.

(Slide)"what? You need a fuckin lesson on how to talk to your man?

(Steph)"No. Please. All I need is you and for you to be happy with me."

She responded in her now standard, meek and unassuming voice. Sadly, there seemed to be no trace of the once fiery young woman that Moe loved. Her spirit must have been broken right along with her heart. Sometimes love isn't always a beautiful thing, in terms of the ones that you've lost and the ones that you've settled for. She always wanted a love that she could enjoy and fight for, but wound up with one that she may have to fight with in order to get out of. Hopefully, her jaw wouldn't turn out to be made of glass, like her heart was. Only bad times would tell.

Honeymoon is Over (Flashback)

(Steph)" He wants me to move in with him."

(Cherry)" Move in? That's kinda quick. You must got that bomb-ass coochie. Got a nigga wanting that live in ass."

(Steph)" I don't know though. My mom says I shouldn't and I know Moe will Trip out over it."

(Cherry)" Yeah, he's gonna trip over it, since you know you're the girl of his dreams and all that good shit. But hell, how many chicks around here got a dude like Slide wanting them to share their space. He's really feeling you."

(Steph)" Like you said, I'm that chick. He knows a good thing when he feels it wrapped around his dick. And my Moe will get over it. He'll forgive me like always."

(Cherry)" So what you gonna do?"

(Steph)" What do you think I'm gonna do? I ain't no dumb bitch. I'm gonna move in with that paid nigga and keep his balls empty while I fill my pockets and shine like the star I was born to be."

(Cherry)" I know that's right."
The conversation ended, at least out loud anyway. But in a part of Stephanie's mind

located way in the back past logic, on the other side of hesitation and slightly behind common sense, the thought that this might be a bad decision lingered barely noticed. And as the sun swallowed her silhouette in the distance, the young woman walked quickly toward a fate that so many of the women raised in the belly of a heartless Public Housing Project fall prey to.

Break

Slide lived on the second story of a two family house located just behind the Lafayette Gardens Housing Projects, on the Woodward Street side. The outside of the house was painted a very somber and subdued green that was a bit out of character for a Ghetto Superstar. The inside of the apartment gave off the clear impression that a man with no steady female or relationship connection lived there. It was by no means impressive, but it would be soon enough once Stephanie added a woman's touch. The young lady viewed it as a challenge that she was willing to undertake. She was very eager and prepared to make as much of his world hers as she could.

On the second day that Stephanie Brown had moved into the smaller than expected but well furnished apartment, she was aggressively reminded that her relationship was destined to be much less than perfect and very different than expected.

(Slide)" Steph! Steph! Wake the fuck up!" Said the angry drug dealer as he pulled the covers off of his girlfriends sleeping form causing her to fall to the floor, with a heavy thud.

(Steph)" What? What the hell?"

(Slide)" Where the fuck my breakfast at!? Bring a bitch up in my house and she don't even know what the fuck to do."
(Steph)" What are you talking about? And who

the hell you calling a bitch?"

Slide's knuckles collided with her cheek and stole the fire from her words. She sat there half naked on the floor and stared up at the man who ambushed her and interrupted her sleep. Her mind spun like crazy trying to make sense of it all. Then as suddenly as his knuckles had landed against her face, his fist had grasped a handful of her hair. He lifted her from the floor and dragged her through the apartment into the kitchen and then slammed her bottom into one the stained wood dining chairs. She sat there with her rump stinging, her scalp raw and her tracks loosened by the exchange. It was profoundly fitting that she was sitting at the island in the middle of the kitchen, since at that moment it was how she felt. Deserted by common sense and alone on an island with a man that frightened her terribly.

(Slide)" Now get this straight Bitch. You ain't no fucking queen in no damn castle that's gonna be laying around all day, spending up my dough and acting like she don't know her place."

(Steph)" My Place?"

(Slide)" Bitch. You better shut the fuck up before I punch you in that smart ass mouth of yours. Don't talk while I am talking. Learn how to fucking listen."

Stephanie stopped speaking and sat there in amazement as she listened to all of her required daily chores and her girlfriendly duties. (Slide)" Every morning you need to get up before I wake up and fix my damn breakfast. And I want some different shit every day. And it better taste good as hell too or that's an ass whooping. Then you need to pick out something for me to wear and iron that shit. No creases in my jeans either. Then wake me up with a nice ass blowjob. And I mean a nice ass blowjob too Bitch or I will beat your ass. And keep that little bastard quiet too, cause if she wakes me up at night, you got a problem. And last but sure as hell not least, I'm gonna show you how to weigh and bag up my product. You got it?"

Stephanie sat there for a second and tried to make sense of it all, but couldn't quite get her mind around it. So she did what most battered women do unfortunately. She swallowed her pride, nodded in agreement and learned her place.

Stephanie talking to herself in the mirror

(Steph) "Why do I stay with him? He is just a bully. He just wants to hurt me. He doesn't love me. He just loves to fuck me and call me his girl. I'm the big prize to him. But then again, maybe I don't deserve any better. Especially after how I treated Moe for all of those years. They do say, what go around come around." This just fate gittin even with me foe breaking Moe's heart. But it hurts so damn bad. I don't know how much more I can take. Something has to make it feel better. Something."

The lost woman sat in front of the mirror wondering what to do and what to feel. Asking if the pretty white powder in the glad bag would help it go away. She'd always wanted to know how so many people could lose themselves in their own personal glad bags, needles, viles and pipes. Stephanie used to think that life could never get that tough. It could never possibly be so bad that you'd freely give yourself over to oblivion and give up hope. Becoming a zombie and using death like a crutch. Making limbo their new place of residence. Becoming fragmented images of their former selves. She was tempted to lose herself, but refused to crumble so easily.

(Steph) "I could never do that to Joy. And what would Moe think about me? Hold up, what am I worried about? He has enough to think about, with Keyla in his life now. I'm probably just a not so good memory to him, after what I put him through."

Stephanie believed the sadness that was now filling her heart and slowly stealing her spirit was her punishment. It was fate punishing her for undermining its design. Moe once told her that fate was cruel. He was right. She didn't know what he meant then, but it's all too clear now. She took her best friend for granted and ignored his heart. Now someone else has it and him.

Keyla had been her friend. Someone that she could rely on and confide in. But now all she was to Stephanie was an obstacle. A 5 foot 7-inch barrier between her and Moe. A parasite who would suck the life, love and the compassion out of her favorite person, if she let her and did not do everything in her power to prevent it.

(Steph) "No matter how hard I try to get past it, I can't. I just cannot accept them as a couple. I know that he loves me more than her. He's just trying to do the right thing, like always. Damn, I love that about him. No. She just don't deserve him. Besides she don't need him half as much as I do. Damn, so why does she have him?"

(Cherry) "Hey Steph, what's up girl? What the fuck happened to your eye? Shit. I don't even know why I ax that. That punk-ass nigga Slide is beatin you girl. You don't need no nigga like that. He just trying to make you ugly so no other nigga try to talk to you. Somebody need to kick that mother-fucker's ass again, like Moe did when he tripped on you that first time."

Cherry stopped abruptly, because she knew that the subject of Moe was off limits. But to her surprise Stephanie didn't flip out.

(Steph) " Yeah I know. He don't treat me right. I'm not his girl; I'm his property. I'm just some bitch he can punch around and then make suck his dick."

(Stephanie started to cry and her friend held her.)

(Steph) "I don't know what to do."

(Cherry) "You need to leave that nigga alone or kill his ass, one or the two. That's what you need to do. Stop letting that man punch you like some damn punching bag, when you know you worth more than that. "

(Steph) "I don't know. Maybe I'm getting what I asked for, you know. Especially after what I did to Moe."

(Cherry) "Don't talk like that. Don't no woman deserve to be beat by no man. That shit just ain't right. You need to start loving yourself again or at least start hating the nigga that deserves it. Shit, so what you made a mistake and hurt someone whom really loved you. It happens. And so what you feel like crap now. I feel like crap inside too sometimes, but I will be damned if I let some sorry excuse for a man beat me up every time that his day don't go so good."

Stephanie knew that her friend was right, but just couldn't get past the fact that her heart was broken and it was probably all her own fault. So, since she didn't have the heart to hurt herself physically, while in her state of self-pity, she let Slide handle the rough stuff.

After talking to Cherry, it hit home that maybe she does deserve better. Maybe love is what she needs? She needs to love herself again and also convince Moe to love her again too. She would do whatever was necessary to make it happen. She needed a plan.

(Steph) "What's the stuff that makes you hurt inside? You always seem so happy."

(Cherry) "It's just a lot of things that happened when I was a little girl, before my father left. I don't really feel like talking about it. It doesn't matter so much right now any more any way, you know." Cherry said with a shaky voice.

(Steph) "Of course it is important. Have you ever talked about it before with anyone? You know, like you are saying to me. You just let it out and get it off of your chest. Put the blame where it is supposed to be and take it off of your shoulders."

(Cherry) "Some things just ain't that easy to talk about. You know. Some secrets are better off left in the dark. Besides, I don't want you to look at me funny or side ways, you know." Cherry said in a very dejected tone of voice. A shroud of shame and guilt came over her face. The pretty young woman became so sad.

(Steph) "It's ah'ight Cherry. You know that I am yo girl and I love you right? And that I would never make fun of anything about you. Especially, something that could make you so sad. But if it is bad enough to make you that depressed, maybe we should go somewhere and get it out of you. Come on with me."

Stephanie put her arm around her friend and led her toward the park. She could feel her shaking. It was like the vibrations started in the core of her very bones. It had to be something really and truly terrible in order to make her tremble like that. So her friend was determined to get her to open up and talk about it. Whatever it was needed to be let out into the open, otherwise it would continue to secretly eat her up from the inside out.

Secrets

(Cherry) "Steph, you gotta promise not to tell nobody. Not anyone. This shit that I am about to tell you is real ill all real personal and I am not real proud of it. So promise me you won't ever repeat it."

(Steph) "Cherry, you know that you my girl and you can tell me anything. We done been through too much shit together. So, of course I promise girl."

Cherry sighs, takes a deep breath and then with shame filled eyes, begins her story.

(Cherry) "Well, the first thing I remember is how my daddy used to have these parties for him and his friends every pay day. They would all come to our house and bring their kids and stuff to eat and drink. They played the music really loud, played cards and drank a whole lot. I loved those parties. Me and the other girls would get quarters, get to sip their drinks and they didn't even seem to care that we were partying with them. It was so much fun. That went on for a while, but then the parties got crazy. People started smoking weed and doing other drugs. They started playing strip poker or just walking around half dressed or not dressed at all after a while. At first I was a little afraid, thinking that I would get in trouble, but my parents never said anything. They just let me stay there and roam around free."

(Steph) "What the hell do you mean they just let you roam around free in a house full of naked adults, both men and women? That shit is sick. How old were you and the other girls?"

(Cherry) "Well, by the time that every body was getting naked, I was the only child there. Every one else had stopped bringing their kids. It was crazy. I mean they acted like I was not even there. I mean there they all were, my mother, Miss Jordan, Mrs. Wilcox and every other lady in the place, walking around butt ass naked with the men watching them and touching them.

Then all I remember is turning around one day and seeing my daddy walk right passed my face with no clothes on. His dick was so big. I was 8 or 9 years old and it was the first one I had ever seen. I was so nervous and shaky, but I could not stop starring at it. It was so big and so beautiful and I wanted to touch it so bad. I know that it sounds nasty and crazy and slutty or whatever, but I could not help myself."

Cherry said, as she blushed really hard. And unknown to her friend, she was getting excited by the memory of her fathers manhood. Her pussy moistened and she wet her panties, but never said a word. How could she tell her friend about her reaction when it was caused by an incestuous situation?

(Steph) "Hold up. You are fucking telling me

that the first dick you ever saw was your daddy's and your mother was right there? Cherry? Did anything other than you watching ever take place?"

Cherry started to continue her story but the look on her friend's face made her ashamed, so she lied.

(Cherry) "Nah that was it. Nobody molested me or raped me or nothing like that. I just got to see the human body at a very early age. It was no big deal. Let's get back to you and your situation. What are you gonna do about all those feelings that you have all bottled up inside about Moe and Key?"

(Steph) "I am not really sure. But I am going to do something, because it is killing me to watch them walk around like fucking newly-weds or some shit. That shit really burns me up. I know that I shouldn't, but I really want something bad to happen and mess up their good thing."

(Cherry) "That's kind of foul girl. He is supposed to be your best friend and she is one of your tightest girls."

(Steph) "Yeah. So why are they sleeping with each other knowing how I feel about the situation. If they were really my friends it would not be like this. If she was really my girl, then she would not have slept with my Moe."

(Cherry) "I don't mean to rain on your parade, but you talk like none of this is yo fault. Like you didn't practically push the man that you apparently loved into the arms of another woman, because you were always fucking someone other than him."

Stephanie knew that Cherry was right, but deep down inside she could not get passed the fact that her love for Moe deserved to be expressed to him, before it wasted away. Her love for him was nearly as big as her love for Joy, so she had to have him. She just had to have him.

The Plan

One unseasonably cool summer morning, Stephanie decided to sit and wait for Keyla on the steps of Keyla's building. She wasn't really sure what to say, but knew that something had to be said. The two young women had been too close for too long, not to be able to talk things out. Besides, it was a huge part of Stephanie's plan.

(Steph) "Hey Keyla, how you doing?"

(Keyla) "Fine. I guess. But why are you talking to me all of a sudden? I thought you hated my guts." Said a really surprised and skeptical young woman.

(Steph) "I never hated you or Moe. It just all happened so quick and unexpectedly, you know. It was a huge surprise."

(Keyla) "For you and me both."

(Steph) "First I realized that I loved him and then decided to tell him and be with him. I felt good. I was so happy. I just knew that everything was gonna be beautiful. But then it just all blew up in my face."

(Keyla) "I know. I know. And I feel really bad. It was so messed up. The timing, the whole everything. And I know I sounded and acted like a selfish bitch, but he just blew me away and I couldn't help myself."

(Steph) "But I mean how did it start? Did you chase him? Did he chase you? I mean, I still cannot understand how it happened. "

(Keyla) "To tell the truth, it started for me about 6 months or so ago. You remember when Jeff treated me like crap and messed me over for that Shakira chick from Booker T."
(Steph) "Yeah, I remember that."

(Keyla) "Moe was there for me. He stayed with me the whole night and never judged me once. He just held me and was so nice to me. He was the first and only actually nice guy that I'd ever met. You were so right about him. When I looked into his eyes and saw how soft his heart was, I started falling for him. But I kept it to myself, because of ya'll situation and because I was embarrassed. But ever since that night, I have been wondering what it would be like to have the love of a man like Moe. Steph it was never the kind of thing like you might think. I never set out to hurt you. I never in a million years wanted to hurt you. I mean, you my girl and we been through too much."

Keyla begins to cry during her heart felt conversation with her friend. She was just so happy that they could talk again and be civil to each other. Stephanie was too, but deep down inside she knew that their friendship was different now. And although it would be the right thing to do, she would never forgive her friend. How could she forgive the woman who made Moe break her heart? Even though she accepted some of the responsibility, ultimately in her mind, Keyla and her always-open legs were the deciding factor! And her heart was split in two right now, with no visible chance of healing in sight. So how could she not be mad at her friend? How could she not hold a grudge? Wouldn't every woman resent the person who robbed her of the opportunity for true love?

(Steph) "Come here girl. It's o.k. I might not be completely over it, but shit I really miss my friends. We been too good a friends for too long to let a man come between us, even if he is a really good man.

(Key) "I can't even tell you how sad I have been about this whole thing. I'm in a relationship where I should be extremely happy with a wonderful man and I should be able to share my experiences with my girls."

(Steph) "Yeah, you are right. Let's just be cool again. Key I am sorry about everything that I said. You know that I love you too girl and would never want to hurt you either."

(Key) "Me too Steph. You have always been good to me and I swear that hurting you was the last thing that I ever wanted to do."

In her mind Stephanie knew that ever this exchange they should be friends again, but in her heart there was too much pain and confusion. She was in an abusive relationship with Slide, while Keyla's unworthy ass was being loved by the man of her dreams. To her that was no where near fair and her heart was bloodied by their love now, so somebody had to pay. Somebody had to feel what she was feeling. But for right now, she would smile and hold her friend.

(Key)" Steph this is great. We need to hang out. We should go snatch up Cherry and do our girls on the block thing. Bring the baby too, because I miss that little chick so much. I can't wait to tell Moe."

Steph)" And Key, Is it cool with you if me and Moe become friends again? My life just aint the same without him, you know." Steph say with a deceptively coy tone of voice.

(Key) "Girl, he probably misses you more than you miss him. And as long as you respect that he is my man, y'all can be as cool as y'all wanna be. Aiight?"

(Steph) "Thanks girl."

"Stephanie's Newly Found Excitement"

An overly excited Stephanie rants to herself in the mirror.

(Steph) "You can be friends with him if you respect that he is my man. What the hell is wrong with that bitch? What kinda shit is that? Bitch trying to rub their relationship in my face, while we were supposed to be making up. But that's cool. Her dumb ass just opened the door for me to show her how it feels to lose the best thing in your life. I'll show her ass. Fucking trifling heffa. But it is gonna take some work and planning. Shit, I'll just do what Moe always says and be patient and perceptive. I'll plant a few seeds of confusion and then wait for problems to grow, while the whole time consoling both of them. Setting the stage for a great performance. And at the end of it all, Moe will be my man and Key will know how it feels to be totally blind sided and betrayed by your best friend.

Slide Comes Home

(Slide) "Stephanie! Where you at girl? You better be here too."

(Steph) "I'm here, so stop yelling!"

(Slide) "Bitch, what the fuck you mean stop yellin? This my motherfuckin house. You better watch ya mouth and remember who the fuck you talkin to before I break ya motherfuckin jaw."

(Steph) "Nigga I am sick and tired of you always yelling at me and threatening me all the damn time. Motherfucker, if you hate me so much and think I'm so worthless, then why are you wit me? Why you always fucking me then?

An enraged Stephanie runs toward an obviously stunned Slide with her fists clinched and her nostril flared.

(Steph) "Then leave me the fuck alone and get the hell out of here. I'm tired of you always yelling at me, beating on me, fucking selling drugs around my baby, cheating with every scuzzy loose ass bitch on the block, and..."

(Slide) "Shut the fuck up!" Slide says as he slaps the saliva from her mouth.
"I do what the fuck I wanna do and answer to nobody. This is my goddam house and you just

some bitch with a kid that I let fuck me. So get that shit right, bitch"

With a stinging lip and glassy eyes, Stephanie runs from the room. Too angry to angry to cry but liberated enough to do something about it this time. The young woman's heart raged while her blood boiled, as she ran into the kitchen and went directly into the knife drawer. She clutched a well crafted piece of metal that could easily cut out a man's heart or cut his throat from ear to ear.

(Slide) "Come back here bitch! Don't make me chase you."

(Steph) "Fine! You want me? Come and get me motherfucka!"

She faced him with eyes that cut like broken glass on unsuspecting flesh and in her hand was a weapon that could change everything in an instant with a single thrust. And in her rapidly beating heart, she had the determination to use it. He froze and stood captive in time and space, because his death was evident in her gaze. Slide was afraid.

(Slide) "Baby. Am I that bad? Bad enough for you to want to kill me and shit? I know that I aint right some times, but I don't deserve to die love. So, why don't you just calm down, take a deep breath and relax your pretty little nerves. We really don't need to take it that far, you know baby."

A nerve wracked Slide automatically began to do what he always did. Let his slippery tongue protect him from the anger of a woman. It was like second nature to him, to slip into his sweet and lowdown mode. Where he would use sugar coated words to cover up his sneaky underhanded ways.

(Steph) "Shut up motherfucka, not this time. Stop wagging that tongue before I cut that shit right out of your Godforsaken mouth."

Slide clammed up and kept his eyes glued to the stainless steel blade in his girlfriend's hand. He was sweating and huffing and puffing, while his mind raced at about a million miles a minute. He stood there biding his time and waiting for his opportunity. The chance to shove that blade in her pretty face and scare the shit out of her. But suddenly Stephanie screamed and broke Slides concentration.

(Steph)" I can't fucking take this shit any more! If you ever in your God-forsaken miserable life put your hands on me again, you're a dead man. I don't care if you beat the shit out of me, or even if you break all of my fuckin' bones. None of that shit will matter if you don't make sure I'm dead. Because if I'm still alive, yo ass won't be for very long."

Then the young lady storms out of the

apartment with child in hand. She headed straight for Cherry's house. The time had come to set it all in motion. Everything that her heart was ordering her to do and her mind was telling her would be impossible. The incident had fanned her flame of hope and transformed it into a burning desire.

Sweet Tasting Cherry

(Cherry)" Hey, Stephanie. What's wrong with you girl? What that nigga done gone and did now? He fighting you again? That is one sorry ass piece of man."

(Steph)" He tried to flip on me, but I couldn't take that shit no more. So, so I ran in the kitchen and got a big ass knife."

(Cherry)" Holy shit! Did you kill that sorry muthafucka? Ahh damn. What the fuck have you done? You should have just left that nigga like I been telling you. Just took Joy and left his sorry, pretty drug dealing ass alone."

(Steph)" No I didn't kill him. I really really wanted to, but I didn't. I didn't even cut him, but I could. And if he ever comes at me wrong again, I will kill his ass."

(Cherry) "You need to leave that sorry nigga alone before you end up in jail and shit."

(Steph) "That is so fucking true. You figure, if I kill him and get locked up, then what about Joy. And if I don't kill him then my ass gonna end up dead. And either way Joy ends up being just another kid with no parents."

(Cherry) "And we aint trying to let no mess like that happen, so, you need to get out of that situation as quick as you can girl."

(Steph) "Yeah, I know. Damn... I have so much to think about and even more to do. So for starters, is it alright if me and the baby stay here tonight? I can't go back there. No right now, I still feel like I could kill that nigga."

(Cherry) "Sure you can. It's no problem. My mother won't mind."

(Steph) "Thanks girl. You are the best. I'll go and stay with my mother tomorrow."

The night was cool and unusually peaceful. Most of the world was asleep and the part to it that wasn't resting had an agenda. Joy and Lorna were in bed, while Cherry and Stephanie were still awake and reminiscing with a bottle of Alize.

(Cherry) "So on a real note girl, how you doing? You ok?"

(Steph) "Nah, I couldn't be worse. Seeing as how one of my best friends is probably getting deep dicked by the man I love right now. Scank ass hoe. I fucking really hate her right now. I could poke her big brown ass eyes out. He probably only with her for her big tittees and her fat ass."

(Cherry) "Yeah, nice guys need pussy too."

(Steph) "But shit my ass and titties are just as nice, if not fucking nicer than hers. Hell look at my shits, these bitches are pretty as hell."

Steph pulled her nightgown up over her head and slung it to the floor. Then she stood there cupping her size 36C's with the big perky nipples.

(Steph) "Man, if I was a nigga, I'd want to suck these mothafuckers my damn self. And let's not even talk about this perfect ghetto booty that I got. Fellas be driving they cars up on the side walk and shit, when I cross the street."

She stood there naked pretending to be drunk, and hoping that her performance would have the desired affect. Her girl friend sat there staring hard but saying nothing. Stephanie could see the desire in her horny friends' eyes. And she would take full advantage of it. So with a quick movement, she grabbed Cherry's hands and put them on her breasts.

(Steph) "Aint those the softest damn titties you ever felt. They feel like Charmin don't they? And feel this ass. If you was a guy wouldn't you want to see that ass bent over and bouncing?"

(Cherry) "Girl why the fuck you got me feeling you up? You know I am a horny bitch. You better put them pretty ass guns away, before my pussy gets any wetter than it already is girl."

(Steph) "For real. Looking at me is making your shit wet? I don't believe you. You just trying to make me feel better?

An embarrassed and inebriated Cherry got up off of the couch and turned to walk away. But before she could escape, a still completely nude Stephanie walks up behind her and grabs hold. Then she cupped one of her friends breast, while her right hand slid down inside of Cherry's panties. Her middle finger slipped slowly and aggressively along the line of her long time friend's vagina. Moving from front to back, parting her lips and then from back to front with an easy determined circular trip taken around her clit. Cherry through her head back and sighed and then Stephanie whispered in her ear.

(Step) "I'll lick yours, if you lick mine."

A stunned Cherry pulled her friend's hand away, turned to face her and then kissed her like she had secretly always wanted to do. She kissed her girlfriend with a tenderness that neither one had ever shared with a man. Their tongues danced together, sharing a liquor-laden waltz that they would never tell anyone about.

(Cherry) "I won't tell, if you don't."

(Steph) "Just take off those clothes and make me cum please. I just really need to cum right now."

(Cherry) "Are you sure you want to do this?"

Before Cherry could say another word, Steph was sucking on her small perky nipples and sliding her panties down to the floor.

(Steph)" I have never done this before, so I hope I do ok."

(Cherry) "I have, so let me show you how it's done."

Cherry was masterful. Her tongue moved with grace and purpose. She held her friend's legs down as wide open as possible, while she taught Steph's clitoris the alphabet. And by the time she reached the letter S, Steph was moaning, groaning and convulsing from her first multi-orgasmic experience. The young woman was a fast learner and also very innovative. She used ice from her glass on Cherry's swollen nipples while she gently sucked her equally swollen clit, like a baby does its bottle.

The scene was raw, arousing, satisfying and relaxing. It was also one that the two young women would repeat eagerly and often. The two women still loved dick. They were just less curious now and satisfied more often. For Cherry it was something new and exciting; however, to Stephanie, it was just a necessary evil that happened to feel pretty damn good.

"THEY MEET AGAIN"

(Moe) "Hey Steph, how ya been? Is everything okay with you and Joy?"

(Steph) "I'm good. The babies good. I've just been trying to cope and keep it moving. You know. Especially since me and Slide don't kick it no more."

(Moe) "For real? I don't mean to pry but, what happened. I didn't think you would ever leave him."

(Steph) "It was never that serious. It just took me a little while to stop being stupid. I was never in love with him. He just filled all the shallow prerequisites that I had."

(Moe) "Yeah I know. I remember. How did you say it? He was your ghetto super star and your status symbol."

(Steph) "Yeah. I was stupid. You don't have to rub it in. I just want to know one thing. Are we still friends or do you hate me too much?"

(Moe) "I could never hate you Stephanie. It's just not possible. We are just two people who are in two different places in their lives. That's all it is."

(Steph) "But it didn't have to be like this. Shit it still doesn't have to be this way. With a single phrase you could change both of our lives. You just don't want to."

(Moe) "It's not that simple anymore, Love. And you know it. There are still three people in this equation."

(Steph) "No Moe. That's where you're wrong. This whole thing has always been about you and me. Slide never really mattered and Keyla is only in your life because you are a man who like every other man needs pussy."

(Moe) "You are so fucked up. Excuse my language, but you got some serious fucking nerve. First off, my girl is so much more than just pussy to me. She listens to me, we do silly things together, and even if we don't love each other yet, we both love the connection that has formed."

Moe's last comment hurt Stephanie so bad, that it retraced the crack in her heart. An old, dressed up wound sliced open again by the callous words of a wonderful man. Her disdain and hatred for her friend grew with every syllable. In Stephanie's mind, it was as if Moe's tongue was digging Keyla's grave.

(Steph) "Damn Moe. It felt good to throw it in my face didn't it? OK so now what? You made me cry again. You got your chance to throw it all back at me. But now what? These tears don't matter anymore. I have been crying over this whole thing for months now. But I want you to tell me one thing. Just do me one little favor. Tell me to my face, that you do not love me and that the idea of you and me has never crossed your mind over these past few months. If you can do that, I will leave right now, give ya'll my blessing and bury my love forever deep inside my heart."

Moe stood silent and stared at the woman of his dreams who was as beautiful as ever, if not more so now. She was begging him to let her be his everything and he was at a total loss. The young man had no clue what to do. Should he be stone hearted and hurt her like she did him? Should he twist the dagger that was obviously buried in her heart? Maybe he should say nothing and keep her guessing and wondering, like she had done him for so long? Or should he just give in, tell the truth and finally live the dream?

(Moe) "Steph, I just don't know what to say. It's just not that easy anymore, Love. There are just too many variables. Maybe how I feel about you can't matter so much anymore? Maybe all of this turning out the way that it did meant that, that particular love was supposed to die hard?

(Steph) "And maybe I needed to see you with my best friend and hear my heart break, in order to view things more clearly? Maybe I deserved to be beat down, kicked, raped and bloodied by a bully? Maybe his anger was necessary to show me what true love was? I am far from perfect and even further from being happy. But at least I finally learned something, even if I did learn it too late. I now know that good guys really are hard to find and bad guys for what ever reason, are hard to let go of."

Stephanie trembled and burst into tears again. She needed him. She wanted him and she would beg him if she had to.

(Moe) "No love, you didn't deserve any of that. All you've ever deserved is the best."

(Steph) "That can't be true Moe. Because why did they happen if I didn't deserve for them to happen? I 've made horrible choices that have ruined my life and I am only 21 years old."

(Moe) "It's true that your choices have not always been sound, but even still every woman deserves better. Especially a woman like you, Stephanie."

(Steph) "Why me especially. I aint nothing great, I aint never do anything to make a difference. Shit, I aint nothing special. I 'm just like all of these other loveless, baby factories around here. Yeah, I might look good, but how long will that last and how far will that take me."

(Moe)"Man, Steph you really don't get, do you?"

(Steph)" Honestly, no Moe I don't get it. So why don't you finally explain it to me. Tell me what made you love me and what makes you believe that I'm so damn special? That's some shit that I would really like to know."

Stephanie was effectively pulling every one of Moe's heart strings. So he gave in and told her what she had asked to hear.

(Moe)" Well for starters, you leave a lasting impression. I mean damn, I can still see that first day that we met in my mind. And it is still as clear as the day it took place. You opened the door to the hallway and almost knocked me down and as you were apologizing our eyes met changing everything. To this very day nothing ever warmed me to the core of my being like being caught in your gaze did that day. And from our first conversation we were so much more than friends. Our spirits collided and we became the victims of something bigger than the both of us. Let me stop rambling."

(Steph)" You're not rambling. You're singing praises to a very needy and confused woman who really needs to hear them. So don't stop. Please."
(Moe)" All I am trying to say is that so much of me belongs to you and that's something that

has proven impossible to shake. You are an exceptional woman who no man could ever hope to be deserving of. You are incredible and you should never forget that or let anyone tell you otherwise. So, now do you understand pretty woman?"

Stephanie could say nothing, even though she'd just heard the most beautiful and wonderful thing that any one had ever said to her. She should have been bubbling over with joy and excitement, but she wasn't. Instead she cried like someone had just killed her child or something. The tears came from way down deep in her heart. They came from that place where only he belonged. That place flooded by a river of pain and despair because its occupant was in someone else's life and in someone else's bed. So she cried for hours and he held her.

Cherry Has Green Eyes

(Cherry)" Where is she? Why hasn't she come back yet? We were supposed to hang out and take Joy to the mall. Yo hold up. Why am I trippin? I know where she is and I should not be acting like she my girl or some shit. Yeah, pussy taste good and being with a woman is fun and feels great, but damn, I love dick. So why am I flippin? Stephanie is beautiful, but she is a fucking woman and I should not be feeling all anxious and jittery over somebody who got the same plumbing that I do. But damn, she really is beautiful and really does taste good.

Now aint this some shit? I'm sitting hear asking myself if she might be feeling the same butterfly stomach mess that I'm going through, on some old dyke shit. I knew that I was into some freak shit, but am I a freakin lesbian? Am I falling for my girl? And if I am, why do I want to set myself up like that? She loves Moe more than anything. She probably loves him as much as she loves Joy. Definitely more than she'd ever care about me. How can I compete against the man of her dreams, if I was digging her? Especially a real nigga like Moe. Let me just get all of this mess out of my mind and go get some dick. Hopefully that will bring me back to reality. Even though I really wish she would hurry up, because I'd really like to see her face."

Cherry at work

Cherry works at The Garment Shop, which is a clothing store located in Jersey City's Hudson Mall located off of Route 440. She is a Co-manager who makes a decent enough salary to live off of, since she still lives at home with her mother Lorna.

(Cherry)" Damn. Gotta keep busy. Gotta keep my mind off of Stephanie's sexy ass."

The young ladies entire morning has been filled with the memory of her encounter with one Miss Stephanie Brown the night before. The encounter that left them both spent and exhausted laying in each others arms with very distinct tastes in their mouths. Her pressure was high and her head was spinning filled with images of forbidden touches and never imagined kisses from a person she's known all of her life. She couldn't contain her thoughts and could not deny her continued excitement because the warm moist feeling between her legs was a constant reminder.

(Cherry)" If I keep thinking about my girl like this, I'm gonna have to steal some panties."

(Cream)" Excuse me. Can I get some service."

Cherry's thoughts were interrupted by the voice of a customer requesting assistance. She welcomed the distraction and rushed to help, but was stopped dead in her tracks by what she saw. In front of her stood Iced Cream a pimp from the other side of Jersey City. A man known for his hoes and his clothes along with a reputation for having a very short temper. He was about six foot two inches tall with a medium brown complexion, with his hair in two ponytails, a full length fox furcoat and at least ten thousand dollars worth of jewelry around his neck.

(Cream)" Miss Lady I need you to help me with something."

(Cherry)" Okay. What can I do for you?"

(Cream)" Bitches, come on in here."

Iced Cream beckoned and two young looking women hurriedly entered the shop behind him. They were not dressed like prostitutes, but he was clearly the boss of them.

(Cream)" These here Hoes, need some clothes."

(Cherry)" Anything or style in particular you ladies looking for?"

(Cream)" Excuse me, but don't ask them bitches. They don't know what they need. Look at how they asses is dressed right now. Can't you see they toe up from the flo up and ain't got no style? Just get these bitches some

suits or some shit like that, with some color, so they can have some sophistication."
(Cherry)" Any particular style or designer?"

(Cream)" Put them in some classy shit, like what you got on. Bitches! Ya'll see her? Now she got some look to her like I do. Bring over about two or three suits like yours and some shirts to go with them."

Cherry could barely contain her laughter at the spectacle that was taking place in front of her, but she kept her composure and did her job. However, the other workers and customers were snickering and pointing in disbelief. The young lady quickly returned with several different colored and nicely tailored women's suits and showed them to Mr. Iced Cream.

(Cherry)" What about these sir?"

(Cream)" Oh, no no no no, don't call me sir. Call my Daddy sir, but call me Mr. Iced Cream or Cream for short. No need for the formal pleasantries, when you are being so helpful to me and my hoes. Okay, pretty lady?"

(Cherry)" Okay, Cream. What about the suits?"

(Cream)" One second Miss Pretty Lady. Can I sit down? These gators is hell on the corns."

(Cherry)" Sure. Here's a bench over here."

Iced Cream looked down, dusted off the bench and paused."

(Cream)" Is this thing clean? This coat cost me a pretty penny and I would hate to see it get dirty. That might upset me."

(Cherry) It's clean. You are the first customer to sit here today and we wipe it down every morning."

Cream flashed his gold fronts, flailed out his coat and then sat like a king positioning himself on a throne.

(Cream)" Them there suits is lovely. Now that's what I'm talking about. Come here hoes and go try them clothes on."

The two prostitutes followed Cherry into the dressing room to change. Cherry was noticeably taken aback by the bruises on the back of the younger woman and could not help but notice the track marks on the arm of the other. These women were obviously the products of hard lives.
(Cream)" Damn! Come on you bitches. Let me see my girls in they new outfits."

The first girl emerged from the dressing room wearing a cranberry colored suit with a cream colored shirt underneath. The color was good on her but it didn't fit her very well.

(Cream)" That is real nice. The color is serious. Turn around for Daddy. Gimme a little spin."
She spun around slowly with her arms stretched out to her sides like Diana Prince used to do when she turned into Wonder Woman.

(Cream)" Hear we fucking go again. You and your syndrome just messing shit up."

(Cherry)" Syndrome?"

(Cream)" Yeah, can't you see her white behind got the syndrome? Noassatall-itis."

(Prostitute)" Daddy stop. I aint got the itis."

(Cream)" Bitch everybody in this room can see you got the syndrome."

Cherry was confused so she had to ask Cream what he was talking about just in case it was contagious.

(Cherry)" What has she got?"

(Cream)" She got Noassatall. No ass at all. Can't you see that hoe ain't got no ass. Her back goes all the way down to her feet. Bitch lucky she a brainchild with big titties or her ass couldn't work with me."

The next one emerged from the dressing room in a lavender suit that fit her overly shapely body like a glove.

(Cream)" See, now that's what I'm talking about. Now that's a sophisticated hoe right there. Okay now how much I owe you Miss Lady?"

(Cherry)" You want both suits?"

(Cream)" Yeah. I want both those suits and them other two you got in your hand. Gimme them shirts too. Oh and get them bitches out them damn sneakers and show them some heals."

(Cherry)" This I can ring up and if they take those two suits off, I'll ring those up too. But we don't sell shoes here."

(Cream)" Okay. But ya'll hoes take them shoes off anyway and leave the suits on. They can leave the suits on can't they Miss Lady?"

Cherry)" Ummm, sure but just let me remove the scanners and tags for you."

(Cream)" Now ya'll move ya'll assess and come on, so we can get some damn shoes for them feet. Hurry up too because I'm tired of shopping and spending my money on clothes for you hoes."

Cream paid the bill, tipped Cherry $50 and left the store with his two employees following closely behind him barefoot with newly purchased suits on.

Walking Home

(Moe)" Damn! As if I wasn't confused enough. Wow, Stephanie is in shambles emotionally and it is all because of me. All because she loves me and wants to be with me more than anything. Holy shit! The woman of my dreams is breaking down openly in front of the world because we are not together.

And she was so beautiful standing there with her tear soaked cheeks and quivering lips. I couldn't take my eyes off of her. This is bad. This is really really bad. I am with Keyla who any man in his right mind would want to be with, but Stephanie has been in my head and in my heart since that first day. And what's worse is that Keyla probably does love me by now and I am not really sure if I can love her. Shit. After Stephanie there is not very much room left in my heart. And when she was in my arms with her body pressed up against mine it was driving me up a wall. Being that close to her and feeling her heart beat so fast beneath those perfect breasts made my mouth water. Then when I let her go it hurt so badly and my legs felt heavy like they didn't want to leave. She looked up at me and I ran. I'd better keep running too, because she is the most powerful force in the world right now and all I am is a man.

Hoe into a Housewife

Slide had been on the run from the cops since his encounter with Stephanie in the alleyway and was growing more and more frustrated by the minute at the idea that she had snitched on him. He could not believe that the woman who had shared his home a short time ago had changed so drastically. She had become one of those women who grab knives and call the police during domestic episodes.

The young black street corner salesman was distraught and a little shaken at the idea that he had lost control of his girl so easily and been humiliated so thoroughly. He was now a fugitive from justice who could not ply his trade. That also meant that he could not make the money necessary to satisfy his debts to his suppliers or even drive around in his most prized possession. Stephanie had undoubtedly informed the police as to the make model and color of his BMW. Hate for her began to fill his heart the way that hate does when fueled by a sense of helplessness and frustration. He vowed that she would pay.

(Cream)" Slide. What's going on family? How's the only brother in the hood with any style aside from myself?" Cream said as he drove up and stopped next to his friend.

(Slide)" Drama."
(Cream)" Kill a man drama or slap a hoe

drama?"

(Slide)" More like kill a hoe drama."

(Cream)" Oh no, you never kill a hoe. Even if she steal from yo ass, you give a bitch a pass. Cause dead ass don't make no cash. Beat a hoe, slap hoe, stomp a hoe out, but never ever ever never cap a hoe. That's loss of revenue. And loss of revenue is never an option."

(Slide)" Well, I aint no pimp, so I think I can kill a hoe."

(Cream)" I hope this aint some old macho ego jealousy shit you tripping on like some kinda bitch. Hope you ain't out here trying turn no hoes into no damn house wife. Pimps and wanna be players young and old need to learn that a hoe is hoe and a housewife is a hoe in an apron waiting to be turned out."

(Slide)" What the fuck are you talking about? A hoe is a hoe is a hoe and a housewife is a hoe in waiting?"

(Cream)" Listen. There three main types of women in this world you got your good girls, yours hoes and your dumb bitches. The good girls are loyal little homemakers who love their boyfriends and husbands religiously and with open hearts. They cook, clean, give birth to rug rats and forgive some indiscretions. They are the foundation of the female race, because most women without the scars of hurt and pain or the stigma of distrust hanging over their hearts are good girls. But every woman has the potential to become either a hoe or a bitch. I mean, you have some hoe – bitches but that's rare since one nature usually overshadows the other. See a woman becomes a hoe when she is either lead to believe or decides on her own that her pussy can get her through life. So she will either use it as a tool in skillful manipulation or designate a price for it's use. Then you got your bitches who are born out of hurt anger and sometimes emotionally traumatic experiences. Just some bitter, spiteful and acting on emotion ass heffas, who ain't got no love lose for the game."

(Slide)" What?"

(Cream)" Okay. Let me break it down a little and give you a scenario. Say you up yo crib consummating a relationship with a new friend, right in the bed you love your significant other in. Then your lady comes home all unexpected like and catches you having relations with your new acquaintance and shit jumps off. See, now a hoe having already secretly committed similar offenses will consider her options before taking any action. And a smart hoe will use your guilt to create a financially beneficial situation for herself. There will be shopping sprees, trips, and maybe even a new vehicle, who knows. But you best believe she will stay married and use her guilt card every chance she gets.

Now a bitch is a totally different animal. If a bitch catches you in her bed, in her house, in some other chick pussy, you better bob and weave and hope your friend can fight. Because a bitch is reactionary and will automatically act out of anger with some form of aggression aimed at either you or you companion, if not both of you. And a dumb bitch will either leave or kill you. I call her dumb because if she leaves, she looses out on revenue and support and if she kills you she can't get no child support from the after life. So she would lose her revenue. And you know, lose of revenue is never an option. And another example of a dumb bitch move is the whole suicide thing. When the bitch kills herself because you were fucking her sister or whoever. Now that's the dumbest shit because you still get to fuck the other bitch and her dumb ass dead. She can't even haunt your ass.

Now do you understand why I would take a smart hoe over a dumb bitch any day? And why you can never successfully turn a hoe into a housewife?"

(Slide)" You are a funny motherfucker. I ain't never heard no shit like that before."

Cream hadn't solved Slide's problem with his anecdote, but it had given his friend a reason to smile. Slide would find his anger again later, but for right now was content to debate the age old question of hoes becoming housewives with his very colorful friend.

Moe and his Momma

Moe is the 23 year old youngest son of a woman that he loves more than anything in this world. Her name is Josephine Jones, mother of seven taken care of by one. She is the person responsible for his perspective on women and the world. By him watching the life she made for him and his siblings on a daily basis while struggling through the existence of a battered woman, Moe learned hard truths. He saw that love can present itself falsely even within the supposed sanctity of marriage. She was never really his father's wife, but more like his sparring partner.

(Moe)" Hey Love, what's up?"

Josephine was Moe's mother and the reason why he called every woman Love as a term of endearment. It was his way of reminding her that he loved her more than anything. He said it to her so often that it stuck and became a part of his everyday language. Any woman of any true significance in his life at some point would be referred to as Love.

(Josephine)" Hey Baby, you just getting off of work?"

(Moe)" Yes ma'am."

(Josephine)" How was your day?"

(Moe)" Interesting as always. You know it's crazy up there at that welfare office around mother's day."

(Josephine)" It's not mother's day Baby."

(Moe)" Nah Love, that's what they call the first of the month, because all of the project mothers are getting the gift of their public assistance benefits."

(Josephine)" That's not nice. And it must be crazy up at your office on a day like today, since people do act like animals when somebody giving 'em something. Like they ain't got the good sense God gave 'em.

Baby, let me ask you something. Is that there Stephanie girl you always got me cooking for, messing with that Slide boy with the red fancy car?"

(Moe)" Yes ma'm. Yes she is."

(Josephine)" Now Morece don't take this the wrong way, but that girl fast. She always messing with some drug dealing hoodlum and breaking my baby's heart. Why you keep chasing after that girl, when she act like she could care less about you in a romantic way? You know I'm not saying this to hurt you, but somebody need to say it. And it may as well be your momma who loves you."

Moe wanted to tell her to mind her business, but he would never show his mother any disrespect like that especially since she was right. So he paused for a moment and thought about the fact that Stephanie was doing to him again what she always did. She was overlooking his obvious love for the hollow affections of a shallow man, who could only offer her disappointment and material things.

(Moe)" Love. She just has this affect on me. I mean, I have cared about her for as long as I have known her. It's just hard to know how special a person is when they don't even know themselves. Ma help me out. Is it me and the fact that I'm a nice guy? Am I a Sucker for Love?"

(Moe)" Baby, don't ever let the fact that some little fast girl's eyes are closed make you doubt the man that you are or what you deserve. You are the nicest, sweetest and most responsible person I know and those are rare qualities in a man. So don't you let no trifling little materialistic stupid girl poison you. You are better than that and I know that one day you will find the love you want and need with a nice girl who will love you and give me grands."

(Moe)" See. That is exactly why I am so glad to be your son. You have always given me so much strength. You just a big old bowl of brown sugar, Love.

The two sat and ate and talked enjoying each others company like always. Moe's heart was hurting but his mother was doing what support systems do when working properly; she was helping him through it

Steph Smiles Through the Pain

(Steph)" this is good. This is really really good. Even though he left and went back to Keyla, this is working out perfectly. Any other man would have stayed, fucked me and never even thought about his girl at home. But not my baby, he is even loyal to a woman he doesn't love because it is the right thing to do in the situation. He really is a good guy.

But he couldn't stop looking at me with all of that love in his eyes. I didn't even know that you could see it like that. When someone loves you so much that their eyes unlock their heart to you. And to hear him say those beautiful words to me like he did. He didn't fool anybody either, because I felt his dick get hard before he pulled away from me. Damn, I can't wait to feel that man in my mouth and anywhere else he wants to put it. But even more than that I can't wait to see what happiness feels like after his love heals my heart. So I guess that it is time for phase two of the plan to be put into action. I need him now and she needs to be out of the way.

Phase II

(Keyla)" Hey baby what's up? I missed you like crazy. Come kiss me and listen to my good news."

(Moe)" What good news?"

(Keyla)" Well, me and my girl Steph, who I have been missing like crazy, made up today. We girls again and it's all good in the hood. Ain't that some good ass news baby? Even though I know it will be a little weird at first, but she'll get used to us and you two will be cool again."

(Moe)" You got it all planned out don't you? Well, I am glad that the two of you are friends again. It was really bothering me that I had ruined such a long lasting friendship. Yeah, that is cool because I saw her today too."

(Keyla)" Oh you did?"

(Moe)" Actually that's where I'm coming from right now. We were talking down the block for a little while and then I came over here."

(Keyla)" So what ya'll talk about down the block?" Keyla said with an obvious attitude.

(Moe)" Nothing much really, we just cleared the air and got some things out in the open."
(Keyla)" Got some things out in the open?

What the fuck you hiding!?"
(Moe)" Excuse me."

(Keyla)" You heard me! What the hell kinda shit you had to get out in the air with that bitch?!"

(Moe)" Hold up. So now she's a bitch, but two seconds ago, before you knew that I had seen her, she was your girl who you had just made up with. But now because me and Steph had a conversation, you got your voice all raised and your gloves on ready to fight. But I am here aren't I? I did leave her and come home to you didn't I?"

Moe quickly and skillfully deflated the situation knowing full well that his lovely girlfriend's temper could have easily gotten out of control and created a volatile situation. Or maybe even forced him prematurely to make a decision that really needs some time to be thought about.

(Keyla)" Yeah baby you're right and I am sorry. But I just can't help the green eyed thing though. Because I know how much she means to you."

(Moe)" its ok love. No apology necessary."

(Keyla)" Yes I do have to apologize. Shit, you are the best thing that could have ever happened to me and I still can't believe it's true. So come in, have a seat and let me get down on my knees and bow my head to my savior."

(Moe)" I'm not your savior, love. I'm just a man."
(Keyla)" Moe you're so much more than just a man to me. You're that thing that I never knew I wanted and that feeling that I never thought possible. So, let me lock this door and give you my body; however you want it, because you already have my heart."

Keyla closed the door and began to take off her clothes, but Moe stopped her. He took her hands, led her to the couch, sat her down next to him and held her tight.

(Moe)" That's not why I am with you. I chose you because you wanted me and I could see it in your eyes. I chose you because I needed you at that very moment as much as you needed me. I picked you because you intrigue me as much as you excite me. So baby, when you're scared, you don't have to use your body as leverage. Not with me. Just tell me how you feel and we'll deal with whatever."

The young lady had no words, so she sat there, held him and let herself get lost in the feeling.

Cherry In The Middle

(Cherry)" Hey Steph, what's up? I was wondering if I'd get to see you any time soon." Cherry said with a relieved sigh. Then she noticed that her friend was upset.

"What's the matter and why are you crying? What's got you so upset, girl?" Said a concerned Cherry as she put her arms around her friend and held her close.

(Steph)" I can't take it Cherry. I need him so bad that it hurts me in the bottom of my stomach every time that I think about him and my body starts to shake every time that I see them together. My eyes are so tired of crying and I'm sick of letting my so-called friend rip my heart out. I have got to do something or I'm gonna go crazy. How could he be with her? How could she betray me like that with no intention of stopping even when she knows how hard it is for me? She's supposed to love me. You're supposed to defend your friends, not hurt them. She's not like you Cherry."

Said and overly emotional and dramatic Stephanie, while never taking her tear soaked gaze from her young friend's eyes, watching closely and gauging her performance in Cherry's expression.

(Steph)" You love me and only want to see me happy. You would never snatch my heart out and throw it back at me. Would you Cherry?" Said a shameless conniver giving the performance of her life.

Stephanie's hand slid slowly up the back of Cherry's neck as she pulled her face closer. The kiss was deep and passionate as their tongues danced slowly communicating unspoken desires and soon to be revealed intentions. Cherry pulled away and then looked at Steph with tear-filled submissive eyes.

(Cherry)" Nope. I would never make you cry and always protect you because you're my girl and I've got you."

And in her head she thought, "Because I love you so much."

Revelations

(Lorna)" Cherry, what's going on with you and Stephanie? You two seem a little too close for comfort lately." Said an always-nosy Lorna, who had just secretly witnessed the kiss between the two young ladies.

(Cherry)" Ma, cut it out. She just going through a real tough time right now and I'm trying to be there for her."

(Lorna)" Uhn Hahn. Just trying to be there for her. So how do you explain the really tender moment that I just witnessed? It looked a lot like lesbianism to me and not friendship. Unless that's how friends support each other now-a-days?"

(Cherry) " I ain't nobody's lesbian. I'm just being a good friend to my girl."

(Lorna)" Girl, don't you fucking stand there and pretend like you don't know what I'm talking about. I just watched my daughter tongue kiss her female friend like she's a damn dyke."

(Cherry)" That's so messed up. For your information I love dick and always have loved dick."

(Lorna)" Alright, Miss Love Dick so much, what about the kiss then? Why was your tongue in

Stephanie's mouth?"

(Cherry)" I don't really know ma. It just kinda happened. It's just that everything excites me and I couldn't help myself. Aiight ma, so leave it alone."

Cherry lied to her mother because she knew that Lorna would never understand. Even though she blamed her promiscuity on her mother anyway.

(Lorna)" all I know is my baby bet not be no damn lesbian. I ain't raise no damn butches."

(Cherry)" Don't you listen? I keep telling you I ain't no damn dyke. But shit whatever I am it's your fault.

(Lorna)" Oh so it's my fault that you a bull-dagger. How you figure that?"

(Cherry)" What? I know you not fuckin tryin to play dumb now! The way you and daddy raised me. The shit that I done seen y'all do. The shit you let him and his friends do to me!"

(Lorna)" Shut up! I don't want to hear that shit!" Lorna said as she slapped her daughter to the ground. "You don't know what the fuck you're talking about!"

(Cherry)" No, I won't shut up. You gonna call me a dyke when I can remember seeing you eat a whole lot of pussy and let all of those strange men fuck you at those parties daddy used to give. And you got the nerve to call me names and judge what I'm doing."

Lorna froze and began to shiver just a little bit at the sound of her daughter's accusations. She barely remembered those days because of all the drugs. But with every word that Cherry spoke, the memories flooded back. She could see it all and for the first time Lorna could feel the shame.

(Cherry)" I remember all of it. Do you? Do you remember a nine year old girl walking through a house filled with naked, drunk ass, drugged out grown ups having sex? Do you remember giving her alcohol and making her take off her clothes so that her father and his friend's could see how big her titties were getting? Putting me on display for a bunch of dirty old men to look at while they touched themselves. Most nights I can still see their drunk faces looking at me like rapists who had just seen their next victim."

(Lorna)" Shut up! I don't want to hear any more. I wasn't a bad mother. I may not have been the best mother, but I wasn't a bad mother. I never beat you or hurt you. Nobody abused you, you always ate, had nice clothes and a good roof over your head. I never hurt you Cherry."

Cherry blew up, lunged at Lorna, grabbed her by the hair and slung her against the wall. Lorna hit her head on the wall and began to cry as the blood flowed freely down the back of her neck.

(Cherry)" What bitch? You saying you never hurt me? You never fucking protected me! All you ever did was use your drugs and walk around like a fucking zombie having sex with whoever was there. And you did it all in front of me. You never talked to me about nothing. You never shielded me from any of it. I grew up knowing that my mother was a drugged out whore. You think that didn't hurt me."

Cherry exploded with a rage unknown to her. Her heart pounded like a jackhammer while all of the different men and women's faces found their way back into her mind. She could feel every hand fondling her young breasts and every alcohol-covered finger rubbing her where no one should have been allowed to touch. She could feel the fear returning and growing deep within her body. But then the shame rushed in too and reminded her of how it felt so good after awhile. She liked being touched down there where it got all wet and tingly. Lorna had never told her to stop or that it was wrong, so she never said no.

(Cherry)" Shouldn't I feel dirty knowing that the first man I ever touched was my father? Shouldn't that bother me? And doesn't that bother you too? Don't you hate him for what he did and what he turned us into?" Said an irate Cherry as she tightened her grip around her mother's throat.

(Lorna)" Cough, Cough. I never let him fuck you."

(Cherry)" Oh and that should make everything better? You didn't keep him from fucking me. He just couldn't bring himself to do it. All those nights when he was holding you down and fucking you with me standing naked next to the bed, it was me that his dick was inside of in his mind. I could see it in his eyes. And what makes it so bad is that I would have let him fuck me. That's why I hate you. I hate myself. I hate him and I'm glad he's dead."

Cherry let her mother go and ran from the room. She ran for Lorna's life, because had she stayed something worse might have happened. Lorna slumped to the floor and cried like the world had just ended. Then she prayed and tried to catch her breath while the blood dripped from her head. Her daughter had nearly killed her, but she wasn't angry, at least not at Cherry. Lorna was upset at herself just then, because her baby was right. So she sat there in that corner, holding her shame close to her heart and continued to cry.

Lorna James

How does a person live with themselves knowing that they are the one thing in this world that their child despises? Lorna James was wondering that very thing at that precise moment. The moment after her daughter had expressed her obvious anger with extreme aggression and tear filled eyes. She knew that Cherry didn't love her like children should love their mothers. The beating that she just received from the young woman made that fact painfully clear. Now here she was sitting in her dimly lit apartment crying profusely and beginning to hate herself a little more every second, while remembering. She could see it all as if it were playing out on a stage right in front of her. Lorna blinked and shook her head but the images remained and grew clearer.

Memories

The music was loud. The apartment was packed with adults ready to shed their inhibitions and indulge their forbidden whims. It also contained one young woman obviously out of place, wide eyed and in danger that she was too young to recognize. There was food, drink and illegal drugs everywhere. It was a scene from a movie that Cherry was too young to see, yet she was the star.

Lorna remembers dressing her daughter in grown clothes to flatter her quickly budding young body. More men paid to get in and brought more drugs because they knew that a 9 year old Cherry would be on the top of their very decadent sundae being offered by her parents like a prize to their guests. Everyone would laugh, joke, drink and use drugs while the little girl was made to bring ice and pass out chips. She was given alcohol to loosen her spirit and persuade her to be less reluctant to sit on the knees of all of her would be uncles, who always placed their hands on her buttocks or rubbed high on her thighs while talking to her. She felt special being at the grown up parties. The men and women gave her money to dance and all seemed to love how she looked so grown already with her big breasts that came early and her noticeable bottom that shook when she walked. She loved the attention, at least that's what Lorna told herself.

However when she looked closer and concentrated on the memories, the horrible mother could see a scared child being forced to show her body and being fondled reluctantly by drug addicts and pedophiles. She remembers slapping her young cheek and making her stand there naked in the middle of a room filled with grown men jerking off and grown women rubbing themselves and making noises. Lorna vaguely remembered seeing Cherry's look of disgust and confusion. She recalled how fixated she was on her father's manhood and how he couldn't take his eyes off of her while he got his dick sucked. But at the time all she cared about was that next orgasm and that next high, her daughter was just a means to an end.

Then there were those times after the parties when her husband would fuck her like an animal to repeated climaxes without ever once kissing or looking at her. Instead he would have Cherry standing in the middle of the room naked or have the little girl sit in the chair across from them with her legs propped up and open. At the time Lorna was too coked out to care or even notice that her husband was a sick and twisted individual who wanted his daughter for himself. And after so many evening and events like those, how could her daughter have turned out okay. How could she be anything but promiscuous and sexually scarred plus confused?

She was a drugged out whore who had raised her daughter to be a whore too. Cherry was right. She was horrible and had hurt her child beyond measure and repair. Lorna began to hate herself too at that very minute. Her tears were flowing uncontrollably and her head ached along with her hurt. Lorna prayed to a God that she knew despised her and had no place in his house for her. She prayed for a forgiveness that she doubted would ever come and begged a strength that she doubted she had. What made the situation even worse was that the addicted and dried out woman knew that once she found her latest high her sorrow would fade like always. The shame would be washed away on the wave of her high and she would be oblivious again. Numbness would replace guilt and Lorna would escape her well deserved self persecution by crawling back into the arms of her illegal sanctuary.

Cherry and Steph

(Steph)" Cherry what's going on? Why are you so upset? What happened?"

(Cherry)" Nothing much. I just tried to kill my mother, that's all. I slammed her against the wall, cursed her out, grabbed her by the throat and squeezed with all of my might."

(Steph)" What the hell are you talking about? You wouldn't do no crazy shit like that. Why would you even think about doing something like that to your mother?"

(Cherry)" Maybe I am a little crazy. Or maybe she's just a drugged out whore that somebody should choke to death."

(Steph)" What the hell is wrong with you?"

(Cherry)" You wanna know what's wrong with me? I'll tell you what's wrong with me. I'm every man's piece of ass and every man's bitch because my parents raised me that way."

Cherry could say no more and her large puffy red eyes had no more tears. Stephanie started to press the issue, but changed her mind. She remembered what they had talked about before and filled in the blanks. A speck of guilt landed near her heart, because now she was no better than every one else who was supposed to had loved Cherry, but instead had used her for their own selfish reasons.

(Steph) "It's O.K. I'm here for you. I will always be here for you".

Stephanie swallowed hard and held her friend as tightly as she could. She loved her like all friends should love each other, but loved Moe more. So her friend's heart would have to be sacrificed and she'd pray for her. That thought made the guilt in her heart grow ever so slightly, but not enough to change her plans.

(Steph)" Cherry it's alright. We both going a little crazy right now. But at least we got each other to depend on. We'll get through this together."

Cherry held her closer than she'd ever held anyone. Stephanie had finally succeeded. She had made her friend fall in love with her and would now use it to her advantage. The young Moe obsessed woman would also use what was learned today if necessary to ensure her success.

Slide Hits Back

(Slide): "Hey Steph" Slide said with a very coy tone as he walked up behind an unsuspecting Stephanie, who was on her way home.

(Steph) " What do you want? Leave me alone."

(Slide) " Oh shit. That's some awfully brave talk for a chick walking all alone down a dark street."

Stephanie realized her predicament and could see the need for revenge in Slides' eyes. However, she wasn't scared. She'd never be afraid of him ever again.

(Steph): "You better kill me, muthafucka!"

(Slide): " Ok, bitch."

Slide hit her with a heavy blow to her mid section that made her crumble to the ground .The punch caught Stephanie off guard and knocked the wind out of her gut. She gagged for air as he kicked her to the concrete.

(Slide): " Where 's your knife now Bitch? Huh! Where's all your tough words at now! Come on, get up, Fuck me up and kill me. Do all that shit you was talking."

Slide kicked the defenseless woman again

hard in the rib cage. The pain hurt so badly, but she refused to cry.

(Slide): " I'm gonna enjoy this you stupid bitch". He said as he pulled the belt from his pants. " I'm about to whip that fat ass real good and then I might fuck you in that ass one last time. Yeah that's what I'm a do. I'm a whip yo ass and then rip yo asshole open bitch."

All of his ranting gave Stephanie a chance to gather herself. And before he could land the first blow with his belt, she kicked him between the legs with all of her might.

Her foot struck him in his manhood so hard that it made him vomit. Slide fell flat on his face.

(Steph): "Okay, you wanna fight, muthafucka? Then lets fight muthafucka, get the fuck up nigga. Oh, you can't stand up can you? Cause somebody just kicked you in yo nuts. My mistake, they kicked you twice. Then Stephanie stomped him in his nuts again.

(Steph): " So you gonna whip me and fuck me, huh? I don't, fucking think so. muthafucka I'm gonna smash your fucking balls up into your stomach. What's the matter, huh can't talk nigga? Now remember this. I fucked you up. Me the no good slut bitch, you tried to control. I did this to you."
Stephanie spit in his face and then left him there lying in a pool of vomit, urine and tears.

Something in her snapped that night dulling the pain and giving her the strength to take Slide on. His reign of power was finally over and she was finally free. The young lady would go home nurse her wounds and refocus her energy on the task at hand. Getting Moe back.

BREAK

(Moe): "So which movie are we going to see, love?"

(Keyla): " Let's decide when we get there. I don't know what all is playing."

As they reached the theatre the two moviegoers noticed a hurt and staggering Stephanie coming down the block from the opposite direction.

(Moe) " Oh, my God Steph are you okay? What happened? Who did this to you?

Moe's heart beat a mile a minute. He was so worried about Stephanie that he forgot Keyla was even there.

(Moe)" Steph, let's get you to a hospital."

(Steph)" No, I'm ok just a little sore."

(Moe)" Did Slide do this? Where is he? I'll kill that sorry muthafucka!"

(Steph)" It's ok, he wont hit me again. Not if he knows what's good for him, he won't."

(Moe)" Ok, but you should at least press charges on his ass just to be safe."

(Steph)" Actually, I like that idea. Will you come with me to the police station Moe? I don't think that I could do it alone, you know" said an overly dramatic Stephanie as she snuck a glance at Keyla.

(Moe)" Of course I will."

Moe walked off with Stephanie leaving Keyla stunned and alone. He was already two blocks away before it hit him that his girlfriend was still in front of the theater. He turned around abruptly, but she was gone.

(Moe)" Shit! I left Key back there by herself and didn't even say anything to her. She is gonna be so fuckin' mad."

(Steph)" Moe you can go. I'll be perfectly fine doing this by myself. My side hurts a little bit but I'm fine. Go get your girl."

Moe was torn but knew that he could never leave a battered Stephanie even if it hurt Keyla's feelings. To see her in pain was making his body ache. She meant everything to him and at that moment he couldn't pretend otherwise.

(Moe)" Don't worry about it. I'll work it out later. Right now you need me and I am not leaving you."

(Steph)" But you left her standing there and said nothing. If you don't go back right now, she will never forgive you. And I'll get the wrong idea. I'll think that I am more important to you than she is. But that can't be true, now can it."

Stephanie already knew the answer to her question and it made her smile. Moe was hers now and she'd never let him go. She never imagined that an ass whopping could feel so good. Slide's ignorant behind had actually done her a favor and saved her some time and energy. So again she smiled and walked off with the man of her dreams holding her close to him. Moe felt bad and secretly hoped that Keyla would understand or at least forgive him eventually.

Break

(Cherry)" Hey Keyla."

Keyla kept walking and said nothing.

"I said hey girl."

(Keyla)" Oh hey Cherry. I'm just kinda fucked up in the head right now."

(Cherry)" Damn, that shit must be going around. What's the problem?"

(Keyla)" Well, me and my wonderful boyfriend were having a great conversation together on our way to see a movie, when we bumped into Steph. And just like that I disappeared."

(Cherry)" What are you talking about, you disappeared?"

(Keyla)" All he saw was her. I mean, yeah she looked a little beat up, but I'm his girl."

(Cherry)" Beat up? Is she ok? What happened? Where is she?" Said a frantic Cherry as her heart began to pound.

(Keyla)" Calm down. I'm sure she's fine since my wonderful, fucked-up boyfriend rushed to her rescue. He ran to her like she was the only thing that mattered." Said an angry Keyla on the verge of tears.

(Cherry)" Key, it's ok. But you know he loves her

more than anything. Everybody knows that."

(Keyla)" But he just left me standing there and never even said a word. He didn't even notice when I left. He probably didn't care."

Keyla's heart sank to the bottom of her soul. She just could not believe what had taken place. It was like an episode of madness or the ultimate cruelty and she felt like it was all her fault.

(Keyla)" I should have known better. Why would I be dumb enough to start hoping for shit? Thinking that a guy like him could ever love somebody like me. He's so damn incredible and I am not really sure what I am."

(Cherry)" What you are is a good person who deserves happiness like everybody else does. You just a little rough around the edges like the rest of us are."

(Keyla)" That's just it. My edges aren't as rough as they used to be. And it's all because of being around him. He makes them smooth."

Keyla's normally unbreakable resolve crumbled along with her infamous heart of stone. The feeling overwhelmed her senses as she burst into tears.

(Keyla)" I love him so much. Everything about him. He makes me so much better than I really am. I like who I am because of him and I don't want to go back to that woman that I was. I never liked her, but I kinda like me now. And it is all because of him. So what will I do with out him?" Said Keyla crying hysterically.

(Cherry)" Key it's ok. Don't break down. Just wait and see what happens next. We all know Moe is a good guy. He'll be back and he'll explain."

(Keyla)" I know. But what happens to me when I look him in his face and see that it's over? Huh, what then?"

(Cherry)" You can't be sure."

(Keyla)" What? I'm very sure. He saw her hurt and all of his love for her came out. He couldn't hide it any more. Hell, I always knew he loved her, but thought that just maybe I could change that if I had the chance. I crossed my fingers and hoped beyond hope that time together would make him love me too. Even if only a little bit."

(Cherry)" Unfortunately, love doesn't seem to work like that. Old loves seem to have more staying power than new loves do. But if it's something that you really want, then you gotta fight for it. You can't just give it away."

Cherry wanted to let Key know that she understood and could empathize with her completely. However, she didn't think that her friend would understand her relationship with Steph. Or understand that she was on the other side of the situation and just as helpless, because she knew that Stephanie could never love her like she does Moe. And as she held her friend, Cherry sighed because she knew that eventually Moe would leave Keyla for Stephanie.

" The Seduction"

The night was winding down slowly as if time was their ally. The stars were bright and the moon was as blue as either of them had ever seen it. Moe could sense a stillness in the air and Stephanie was poised to embrace opportunity. Their footsteps echoed loudly against the concrete and slowly faded away in the distance. They were alone under the shimmering light of an emotional moon.

(Steph)" Thank you again for helping me see this thing through and finally pressing charges on Slide."

(Moe)" No problem Love. I'm just glad that you finally took charge of your life and got away from him."

(Steph)" Yeah, me too. But I know that I've let you down with the whole situation, and you'll probably never forgive me."

(Moe)" There's nothing to forgive. You did what you felt you needed to do in order to get what you thought was important at the time. How can I fault you for that?

His mouth said the words, but he wasn't 100% sure that they were true. They walked along slowly and talked like it had been years since the last time. It was a truly nice moment neither of them wanted to let end. Stephanie's mind raced frantically, from one thing to the next, acting out every conceivable scenario. However, her smile never faltered and Moe never caught on. He was too busy fighting with himself over whether he should follow his head or his heart.

(Moe)" To tell the truth, I never thought you would leave Slide. I was scared for you. I thought you'd either end up dead or in jail."

(Steph)" Yeah, I was scared for me too. And for a good little while, I couldn't even recognize myself. It was crazy how quick things went from good to bad. He went from Super Nigga to sorry ass woman beating nigga over night. Shit, to be honest I'm still a little scared."

(Moe)" Don't be. He'll be locked up soon."

(Steph)" That's not what I'm afraid of. I'm afraid of never knowing and not finding out."

(Moe)" Never knowing what?"

(Steph)" Never knowing us together as more than friends. Haven't you always wondered about that? Well for me, that's all I think about lately."

(Moe)" I know what you mean."
(Steph)" Do you really Moe? Even now?"

(Moe)" Yeah, I do. I know what it's like to

wonder about us."

Moe tried to stop himself but before he could all of his dreams were revealing themselves on the tip of his tongue. Spewing out anxiously for their audience. The young, beautiful and attentive Ms. Stephanie Brown, who would listen to every word. His heart would reluctantly open up one more time for her and let whatever needed to be known, do exactly that.

(Moe)" Steph, I have been scared for so long, about so many things. Afraid that our lips would never meet, or that my fingers would never get to memorize the line of you. Afraid that I'd never know the smell of you, the taste of you, or the squeeze of your excitement. Scared that my next tomorrow would begin without you. Always worried that dreams do die hard."

His eyes never left hers and shown with an intensity she'd never seen from him before.

(Steph)" Moe, you don't have to be afraid anymore. I'm right here, with you, right now. Two feet in front of you, hoping you'll hold me, needing you to love me and wondering what's taking this man so long to kiss me. Actually, I can't wait anymore."

Stephanie put her hand behind Moe's neck and pulled his mouth to hers. Time crept forward as their mouths met for the first time. Moe's heart nearly stopped as the beautiful young woman stole his breath away with the sweetest kiss imaginable. His muscles tensed, his eyes closed and his fingers found the curve of her back that lead to the soft rise of her bottom. And as he picked her up off of the ground, she wrapped her legs around his waste. The kiss was as intense as the birth of a star. The two young people's bodies reacted chemically to one another like the components of a passionate elixir. Passers-by had to look away because the brightness of their connection was blinding.

(Moe)" Wait. Stop. I can't do this. Not like this. Not now."

(Steph)" Can't do this? What are you talking about? You can't do this? After everything that's happened and everything we've been through. Hell, every minute we've spent together, every second, every thought, shit every everything has been leading up to right now. And you can't do this?" Said a hurt, stunned and confused Stephanie Brown standing in front of the one thing she'd always needed.

(Moe)" I can't do this to Keyla. Not like this. She deserves better."

(Steph)" But what about me? You just finished telling me what I deserved and that I'm so special. And the kiss? I know you felt what I felt just then. But you can't do this to your girl? To Keyla, a chick you don't even love. But what about what you're doing to me and to us? Two seconds ago I had my dreams in the palms of my hands and you're gonna throw them back in my face. And just toss me away, again, for her? " Said an overly emotional and very distraught young woman.

" I know you love me! I know you do! I can see it in your face right now. I have always seen it in your face. Behind those big brown comforting eyes, I can see who your heart belongs to."

(Moe)" Steph, maybe you're right, but I told you before this thing is bigger than the two of us and I wont intentionally break Key's heart. Just like I would never purposely do anything to hurt you."

(Steph)" But you are hurting me." Said Stephanie as she ran into her building and into her apartment followed closely by Moe.

(Moe)" Stephanie don't do this to me, please. Don't make this any harder on me than it already is."

(Steph)" Harder on you? Who's the one crying their eyes out? Who's the one about to fall apart? Not you. No. Not you. Not Moe. He has his girl to go back to, his precious Keyla. And what do I have? Tell me, what do I have? Other than my daughter, all I have are bruised ribs and a battered heart. What do I do about that? Huh? Who's gonna save me now that you're some other chicks super hero? What do I do?"

Stephanie turned away from her friend and put her face in her hands as she sank to the floor. Moe kneeled down in front of her and ran his hand through her hair as he whispered.

(Moe)" I've loved you for so long and it is tearing me apart turning you down. All I want to do is wrap my arms around you and make the pain go away. Make you feel better. But, Steph I need you to understand why it has to be like this. Why this is the right thing for right now. I need you to let me do what's right."

(Steph)" And I just need you."

Stephanie stood up, walked to the door, locked it and then turned to him. She wiped the tears from her cheek, kicked off her shoes and pulled her shirt over her head. Moe stood perfectly still, awed by the woman before him. He swallowed hard, she stepped out of her jeans, unhooked her pretty pink bra from Vickie's and then shared her perfectly shaven secret with him as she stepped out of the matching panties.

Moe's eyes never once left her form and the

lump in his throat grew as quickly as the lump in his pants did. Every inch of his body was excited. There she was even more incredible than he had imagined. He could see her nakedness and could smell the subtle hint of her excitement in the air. It made his mouth water. She walked toward him and he retreated until the wall put a stop to his escape.

Then there she was within arms length wearing absolutely nothing and covered in little goose bumps. She was so beautiful to him and completely irresistible. Yet he tried his best to resist her temptation.

(Moe)" Steph, what are you doing?"

(Steph)" Giving myself to someone who deserves me. Touch me" She said as she grabbed his wrists and placed his hands on her face. The young woman then guided his trembling fingertips down along her neck and then across the front of her body. Gently over her breasts, down her stomach and then along her hips and across her bottom. Next she slipped the middle finger of his right hand in between her thighs along the fold of her vagina and then nudged it deep inside of her moisture. Moe shivered along with her and sighed deeply as Stephanie slowly placed his excitement soaked finger against her outstretched tongue removing every drop. Then she kissed him deeply and shared her flavor. His hands found every inch of her while their tongues slid across one another hungrily.

She began to kiss his neck, then opened his shirt and kissed his chest, gently licked across each of his nipples, teased down the middle of his stomach to his belly button and then rubbed her face against his engorged manhood, through his pants. Then with an eager anticipation she released his excitement from it's confinement and gave him a moist blessing from her crouched position. Her right hand squeezed and jerked him aggressively while she nearly choked herself with every thrust. Saliva dripped to the floor and Moe held on tightly to the back of Stephanie's head. He barely maintained his composer as her throat opened up to him.

She stood up, kissed him again and then removed his clothes. He was everything she'd heard and more than she'd expected. Moe turned her around, placed her hands against the wall and then forced her legs open as if he was about to search her form. For a moment the young man hesitated and enjoyed the view while the tips of his fingers journeyed down her back and all around her perfect ass. He loved every inch of her caramel skinned body. Just like he always knew that he would. Next he kissed her back softly barely placing his full lips against her flesh. Steph shook from the inside out and filled with a burning urgency. He loved her ass. It was well shaped and shook slightly when he smacked it. She let out a throaty groan as he grabbed it and spread it wide in front of his face. She leaned forward, got up on her toes and arched her back as he licked skillfully across her asshole and then along the line of her second set of lips.

(Moe)" I love you so much Stephanie."

Moe whispered as he spelled his name against her clitoris with his tongue. Then he picked himself up, raised one of her legs onto the arm of the chair, held her waist, pushed her down just a little more and thrusted his manhood deep inside of her eagerly and repeatedly until the thick evidence of her excitement covered him. The orgasm began at her toes and followed the scream from her mouth.
(Steph)" I love you more."

Stephanie said as she turned to face him and then rose up in his arms while wrapping her legs around his waist. He reached under her legs, elevated them higher and leaned her back against the wall. The penetration was deep and his erection felt like it was made from stone. The episode was long, loud and extremely satisfying. Ending with sweat, tears and the taste of each other's juices in their mouths and then sleep.

Break

Morning has the tendency to come abruptly after an exhausting night filled with pleasure. And reality likes to creep in just after the first rays of sunlight enter your bedroom. Stephanie rolled over and reached for her man only to find a pillow in his place. He had left while she was sleeping and never even said good-bye. Normally, a woman would be devastated by such a cowardly and insincere act. However Stephanie was fine, because she knew he'd be back. She was oozing with the confidence of a woman who was recently empowered. She knew that Moe would do the right thing and tell Keyla and then he would be hers. And even still she knew that even if he did not tell his girlfriend what had happened, she would of course inadvertently let it slip.

(Steph)" This is going to be a beautiful day."

And she laid there basking in the warmth of the Sun's rays and still wading in the remnants of afterglow, Stephanie threw the covers off of herself revealing her nakedness. She closed her eyes, let her fingers wander across her body and remembered every second of their encounter. The young lady squeezed her swollen nipples with moistened fingers and then arched her back as she moaned. Next she rolled over on to her stomach and raised her bottom slightly so that her right hand could find its way in between her thighs. There she found her throbbing clit waiting anxiously to be caressed and squeezed. So she obliged and spelled his name slowly with her fingertips. The orgasm came quickly and lingered for a long moment while it slowly coaxed her back into a deep peaceful sleep.

Break

Moe had left Stephanie's bed almost immediately after the pretty woman had fallen asleep. Knowing that if he had stayed he'd still be there. He sat there in that big comfy chair beating himself up about what to do.

(Moe)" I have seriously fucked up this time. My already complicated life has just gotten more complicated. Why didn't I just stay with my girl and go see a movie, like I was supposed too? Or why didn't I leave when I had the chance to? No, I had to try and save the world like always. And now all I have managed to do for certain is hurt one, if not both of the women I care about. No matter who I choose, somebody's heart gets broken because of me. I have got to go talk to Keyla.

(A knock at her door)

(Moe)" Hey."

(Keyla)" Oh, so you have come to visit me? Keyla, the person who is supposed to be your girl. The one you left standing alone in front of the movie theater last night.

(Moe)" I know it was stupid, inconsiderate and messed up of me and you have every right to hate me. But it just kind of happened and then...."

(Keyla)" Oh, so you just kinda happened to leave your girlfriend, who you've been fucking for the last few months on a cold side street, so you could fix your broken best friend? The same one who wants to be with you and doesn't want us to be together."

(Moe)" Keyla I know you're mad and like I said you have every right to be. But you know the situation and.."

(Key)" What did you say? What the fuck did you just say? I know the situation! Oh, okay. I got it. I'm supposed to understand that you love her and left me standing out in the cold to be with her. Oh, and the other part. The stay out all night, no phone call, oh ummm forgive me for sleeping with Stephanie part." She cringed when the words came out and she hoped that there was a different explanation. " You did sleep with her, didn't you? Finally lived the dream?"

(Moe)" Baby, I... Fuck it, I won't lie. Yeah, we slept..."

Keyla slapped him as hard as she could before he could even finish his sentence. Then she erupted in a flurry of angry, hurt tears. Her voice trembled while she vented.

(Key)" How could you do that? Why would you do that to me? You're supposed to save me. Supposed to save my heart. Supposed to be better than the rest of them. But all you're better at is hurting me. And you did it better than any of those other guys ever could. They never gave me hope or made me believe in the impossible, all they did was fuck me. You made me feel special. Matter of fact, I thank your sorry ass for that. But now the real world is back and everything can return to normal. Moe, the great guy can finally get the girl he's always wanted. Stephanie gets to have her guardian angel back with a few perks thrown in and Keyla gets brought back to her senses. She gets to be alone again."

(Moe)" That's not what I meant. I meant that you are aware of how unexpected and hard all of this has been for me. And yes I made a horrible mistake by leaving you alone like that, but I was so caught up seeing someone that matters to me in pain."

(Key)" Oh, so sleeping with her while still in a relationship with me wasn't a mistake? You son of a bitch! So now true love justifies cheating? It's supposed to be ok?"

(Moe)" No! It's not ok to cheat on your girlfriend. But it's even worse to lie to her and yourself about how you feel. I'm sorry it happened like this but...."

(Key)" But it had to happen.. Nothing can stand in the way of true love. I know. I get it. You don't have to say it out loud. Just leave please. I can't be around your trifling ass right now."

(Moe)" We need to talk about this."

(Key)" Talk about what? I know I'm not your girl no more. I know you fucked her. I can smell her stink ass pussy all over you. Didn't even take a shower to try and hide it. And I have always known that you love her more than anything. I know all this, so shut up about it. I am sick of hearing about the fucking greatest love of all. So do me a favor and get the fuck out."

Moe left quickly with a heavy heart. Yes, he loved Stephanie, but he wasn't ready to jump into a relationship with her and trust her with his emotions. He needed to tell Keyla that, but she wouldn't listen. So he left without saying another word. He'd let her calm down and then he'd come back, because she needed to know some things.

(Moe)" Damn! She wouldn't even look at me. What the hell have I done? I finally got to live out one of my dreams, but unfortunately it was at the expense of Keyla's heart. What can I do? I am not sure, but I have got to fix this. The crazy thing is, I have really enjoyed being her boyfriend."

Break

(Cherry)" So how was it? Did you do it?"

(Steph)" Do what? What are you talking about?"

(Cherry)" Did you finally get your boy? Did you kiss him on those full ass lips of his? Did ya'll do the nasty, knock boots, jump in the sack? You know damn well what I am asking you girl."

Stephanie hesitated for a moment somewhat reluctant to tell Cherry, because she knew that her girl loved her. She wondered to herself if the hesitation was to protect her friend's feelings or just to keep her wild card in tact. So when she finally answered her, the pretty woman chose every word carefully.

(Steph)" Well, since you need to know my business so bad, the answer to your questions is yes. We made long, passionate love under a full moon. It was everything and more than I expected. That man is every inch incredible and so sensual too. You know how when he talks to you his words paint a picture and capture your imagination? Well girl his touch sings to you with every movement. And damn that boy can sing. Hell, I'm still humming his tune.

(Cherry)" Shit, I need to get some of that."

(Steph)" Don't even fucking play like that, girl. One of my so - called friends knowing what my man feels like is already too much. So don't even think it." The young lady said in a heated tone with a very intense look on her face.

(Cherry)" Calm down, you know I am just joking. I know how important he is to you, so you should know that I would never pull no crap like that." Cherry said with heartfelt expression. However in the back of her mind and in between her legs, being with Moe sounded like a good ass idea.

(Cherry)" So forget all of that. Are you guys a couple now or what?"

(Steph)" Yeah, he's mine. He hasn't officially come right out and asked me to marry him or anything, but it's pretty much a done deal."

Cherry cringed at the idea that the two could potentially get married and become a family. It was something that she hadn't really considered before just then. And now it would probably never leave her thoughts.

(Cherry)" So it's that serious? You think ya'll might do the whole marriage thing for real?"

(Steph)" Shit, I'd be lucky to have a guy like Moe in my life in anyway, especially as a husband. Hell, I fucked it up before, but now is my chance to do it right and nothing is gonna keep us apart. I am gonna make him happier than I even know how to do."

(Cherry)" But what about his girlfriend, Keyla?"
(Steph)" What about that back stabbing no good bitch? She done had enough of my man dick. Shit, she lucky I don't snatch her damn hair out her head for doing what she did!"

Cherry could hear the anger in her friend's words and see the need for revenge in her eyes.

(Steph)" All I know is that bitch better let go real quick and real easy, if she know what's good for her ass. He's my man now and I ain't even trying to share none of him with no skank ass hoe trick."

(Cherry)" I hear you. But what if she puts up a fight and won't let go so fast or easy?"

(Steph)" Let's just hope that bitch got a brain under all that weave in her head."

After Stephanie left, the air in the apartment was still and Cherry's mind was racing in every direction. Her palms were sweating, her pulse was racing at an outrageous pace and her eyes were filling with an ocean of tears. She had to sit down to avoid collapsing to the floor. It hurt like her heart had been raked across a wooden board and filled with splinters.

(Cherry)" Calm down girl, you knew it was coming. It was bound to happen sooner or later. Just not so soon." She said while attempting to slow her breathing and regain her composure.

Winds of War

It's said that love comes from a place of softness and good intentions. That may be true, but all too often it ends up in the middle of a battlefield blown to pieces by it's own implications. Making it more tragic than Beautiful.

On a somewhat cool and unseasonable day, Moe ran into Cherry on the corner of Grand Street and Woodward Street while he waited for the #1 bus to Newark.

(Moe)" Hey Cherry, what's up?"

(Cherry)" Hey Moe." Said a surprised young woman whose thoughts were interrupted. " I'm good. Just taking this crazy life one day at a time. You know how it is?"

(Moe)" Yeah I do. Me and crazy are real good friends right now."

(Cherry)" What are you talking about? You should be on cloud nine somewhere looking down on us unlucky people."

(Moe)" Oh, so I guess you heard?"

(Cherry)" I heard."

(Moe)" From who?"

(Cherry)" Both. They are my best friends you know."

The two got on to the bus, Moe paid both fares and then they sat down next to each other.

(Moe)" So you must think I am the worse guy in the world for doing what I did."

(Cherry)" Not really. I know you're a nice guy and everything, but when it's all said and done, you just a man with a dick like the rest of them."

(Moe)" Oh, so I'm typical?" Said a slightly offended Moe.

(Cherry)" No. That's not what I'm saying. I'm saying that no matter how nice, sweet or good you are, when your shit gets hard, all of the blood leaves your brain too. Like all of the rest of them.

(Moe)" Ha, ha. That was cute."

Cherry could not believe how bold she was being. It must be true that love lends courage to the meek of heart when they need it most.

(Moe)" But Cherry it wasn't like that with either one of them."

(Cherry)" Okay, then tell me what it was like. Hell, this is a long ass bus ride. We got time. As a matter of fact, you can start with the whole Keyla thing. How did that happen? You two were always fighting.

(Moe)" Well like you said, I am a man. So obviously all of this time I have been noticing her. She's extremely attractive and her attitude makes her sexy. She walks like a dream and unknown to most people Keyla is a soft touch underneath all of that female thug bravado. She went through some stuff a while back, I loaned her my shoulder and ever since then it was different between us. I don't know if you ever noticed or not, but her insults got less harsh and she didn't yell at me as often."

(Cherry)" Now that is true. when I think about it. She even bit Stephanie's head off one day defending you. But I didn't pay it much mind."

(Moe)" Why were ya'll talking about me?"

Cherry saw her opportunity to throw some water on the fire. It was her chance to fight for Keyla and hopefully undermine Moe and Stephanie's relationship. She knew that it wasn't right, but what made him automatically deserve her heart? She loved Stephanie too.

(Cherry)" Well, Steph was talking about Slide and her plans to be with him when Key just blacked out and started screaming on her about leading you on. Steph said she didn't see you like that so it couldn't really be called leading you on. Then Keyla practically bit her head off, telling her that good guys deserve better than being treated like somebody's lap dog."

(Moe)" For real?"

(Cherry)" Yeah. And then all of a sudden she tried to change the subject, when Stephanie asked why she cared so much bout how she was treating you. It was really weird."

Moe sat silently for a moment taking it all in. Cherry's story unsettled him. He wanted to accuse her of lying but couldn't see any reason why she would. Now Moe felt even worse about hurting Keyla the way that he had by sleeping with Stephanie. Cherry's well-timed disclosure hit its target with great precision. His doubts about building a relationship with Stephanie grew exponentially.

(Moe)" So she never saw me as boyfriend material?"

(Cherry)" Not until she saw you kissing Key that day." Said the nervously convincing young woman as she threw salt into Moe's recently reopened wound.

That last part was a lie, but she was committed to it now. Moe was a great guy, but he was also the competition. She figured that since Stephanie's mind couldn't be changed, she'd have to change his mind. She felt really bad though, because the hurt was written clearly behind Moe's eyes. The idea that Steph had lied to him had never even entered his mind. They had always had each other's backs and been truthful with one another. Or at least so he had thought up until his conversation with Cherry. Just then he wasn't even sure who she was anymore. A bitter taste developed in the back of his mouth that would sour Stephanie's appeal.

(Moe)" She swore to me that seeing me with Keyla had nothing to do with it. I can't fucking believe she'd lie to my face like that and pretend that she had been on her way to talk to me the whole time."

At that moment his emotions were so conflicted that Cherry couldn't tell if he was in pain or just angry.

(Cherry)" Moe don't feel like that. You two have been through entirely too much together. I am sure she had her reasons for deceiving you like she did."

(Moe)" What reasons could there ever be to explain breaking a trust? Stop defending your girl. She treated me like a puppet and I handed her the strings. It's not even her fault. Hell, I let her do it to me."

(Cherry)" Moe relax. The two of you are together now and that should be all that matters. So calm down and let it go."

Moe said nothing. The heart broken, foolish feeling young man just sat there looking out of the window replaying everything that he and Stephanie had ever shared back in his mind. Cherry on the other hand was patting herself on the back while hoping Moe would confront Stephanie and blow everything out of proportion. Then Steph would get upset, break it off before it got started and then she could step in and save the day. Once and for all proving to her girl that her loyalty, love and support were even stronger than Moe's. She'd show Stephanie that some heroes are heroines and that some true loves come from truly surprising and unexpected places. Cherry was very proud of herself. She thought that maybe now she'd have an honest chance to find out what love looks like with the lights on and her legs closed.

Break

(Lorna)" Moe. Moe! What, you got wax in yo ears boy? Don't you hear me calling you?"

(Moe)" Sorry Miss James. My head is somewhere else right now. I didn't mean to be rude. How are you doing?"

(Cherry)" Boy forget all of that. What got you walking around in a fog? Actually, I already know. Which one of those fast assed, big booty girls done put it on you and got you all confused?"

(Moe)" Miss James, no disrespect but I really don't want to have this conversation right now."

(Lorna)" Now I know it's a delicate situation for you trying to handle having sex with two best friends."

(Moe)" What! Was it in the newspaper or something?"

(Lorna)" Practically. The way you been going from one bed to the other. I always said watch out for those quiet ones."

(Moe)' It's not like that."

(Lorna)" Okay, so you're not sleeping with two of the prettiest girls in the projects, at the same time, who just happen to be best friends?"
(Moe)" Well, I,"

(Lorna)" I am not a relationship guru or nothing, but I have had my legs and my heart open to quite a few men in my lifetime. And if I learned anything, aside from the fact that the male ego is fragile, it's that opportunities for real love/lust situations are few and far between. And sometimes orgasms get in the way of the bigger picture."

(Moe)" Oh, okay. I'll do my best to remember that."

(Lorna)" Well then I have done my part and you can go fix this mess."

Moe left the encounter hoping that whatever Lorna had taken would wear off soon for her own good. He had no idea what she had meant and really didn't care. He had more important things on his mind besides the raving of a horny, burned out, nosy old lady.

Break

Eddie's corner store was crowded as always. Filled to the brim with customers needing money orders, wanting to cash checks and anxious to play that number that they dreamed about the night before. Stephanie was one of those dollar and a dream people, who spent $5 a week hoping to win the lottery. Mr. Jennings was in the doorway teetering back and forth cradling his bottle of Thunder Bird like it was his first-born. All of a sudden the whistle in the wind died down and everything went quiet. It was like that moment in a movie when something dramatic is about to take place. Steph turned to see what everyone was looking at. The door opened and Keyla walked into the overcrowded neighborhood store. Their eyes met, their expressions changed and the room filled with cackling, ohing and ahhing. There they stood, best friends since Miss Ivy's first grade class at P.S. #22, looking at each other like sworn enemies ready for war. Poised to rip the clothes off of each other's backs and pull the hair from each other's scalps.

However, on this day the crowd would be disappointed, because there would be no fight. The two women never even spoke to each other. Stephanie would have gladly egged Keyla on with the hope of starting a physical encounter. But her former best friend never even gave her the chance to say a single thing. Keyla turned and left the store almost as quickly as she'd entered it. It wasn't that she was afraid or anything like that. At that moment she just felt more like crying than fighting. So she left before Stephanie could see it in her eyes. It was bad enough that she had stolen Moe away. She would not give her the satisfaction of letting her see how much it hurt.

(Keyla)" I fucking hate her so much." She mumbled to herself as she walked down the block wiping her tears.

" Why she have to fuck him now? Didn't want him until I had him. Now she all of a sudden can't fucking live without him. Well fuck that shit. She gonna have to because I need him more than she does and she don't fucking deserve him anyway. Full of shit ass heffa should go back to her woman beating drug dealer boyfriend Slide and leave my Moe alone. Cause he's mine now and if I can't have him, she sure as hell can't."

She wasn't even sure about the meaning behind her words, but her level of determination was high and coupled with an unsettling level of conviction. Stephanie was no longer her friend and she would soon learn that vengeance is a terrible thing no matter what side of it a person happens to be on. Keyla's tears would dry and her heart would harden if Moe actually chose Stephanie as his companion. But below the anger, she prayed that the little bit of softness in her heart would stick around for a long time, because it felt really good. So she crossed her fingers and went after Moe. To her, he was an opportunity for happiness that might never come around again.

Break

Vengeance

Hell has no fury like a woman scorned or a woman determined to get her man. That can also be said for the conviction of a jealous soul when it first feels the wrenching pain of betrayal. The line between love and hate is far too thin for the faint of heart and too dangerous for the unprepared. Vengeance is mine, says the person who is engulfed in anger and seeing the world through hateful eyes. At that point revenge is not an emotionally driven response; it is a necessity.

Moe woke up this morning with the weight of betrayal on his mind. He was mad at himself for what he had done to Keyla and even madder still at how Stephanie had lied to him and undermined everything that they had meant to each other. He wanted to cry, but could not bring himself to do so. Instead he got up, took a shower, made himself some breakfast and watched the news. He thought that maybe the turmoil and chaos of the rest of the world would provide some distraction. It didn't work very well.

The phone rang.

(Moe)" Hello."

(Steph)" Hello. How is my baby doing today?

(Moe)" I'm fine."

(Steph)" So, why haven't I heard from you? Was I just a cheap trick or a one night stand?"

(Moe)" No. You were much more than that. But I can't do this?"

(Steph)" What are you talking about? You've already done it. You've already been inside of me and showed me how much you care about me. I could see it in your eyes while we were together. So what are you talking about?" Stephanie said in a somewhat raised tone.

(Moe)" Exactly what I said. I can't do this you and me thing. It was beautiful. I'll never forget it, but I don't want to be in a relationship with you."

Stephanie could not believe what she had just heard come out of the mouth of the man she loves. It could not be possible that he was tossing her aside after the most perfect experience she'd ever shared with anyone.

(Steph)" Don't you love me? But it was beautiful. No. This is not right. This is not how it is supposed to be. This is all wrong Moe. You are all wrong about this. We're supposed to be together now, finally. You and me in love in front of the world, just like you always wanted it to be. No! This is all wrong! This is not the dream."

Said a distraught, quickly becoming hysterical Stephanie.

Moe held his breath and stuck to his guns. He was determined not to fall for any more of her tricks or lies. She'd hurt him too much already.

(Moe)" No! I will not do this to myself anymore. I will not give you the power to hurt me any further. So it's over."

(Steph)" But what did I "

Moe hung up the phone before Stephanie could finish her sentence. He felt so bad, but knew that it had to be done like this or else it would never be done at all. And Stephanie exploded into tears. She cried furiously while her heart felt like it was ripping from her bossom. He had never hung up the phone on her before and it shocked her. She would cry for a long time, but then anger would set in followed closely by a need to avenge herself.

Break

It was a late Thursday afternoon in the middle of a very overly warm day, when Cherry and Keyla bumped into one another in front of Cherry's building. Keyla seemed driven and Cherry was bubbly and bouncing. One of the women had hope in her heart, while the other was poised for a battle that she knew was on the horizon.

(Cherry)" Hey Key, How you doing today girl? "

(Keyla)" I'm good. Just got a few things I need to do. You know how it is when you minding your business enjoying your life and then a nasty ass, annoying bug starts buzzing in you ear. Then it just kills your whole groove and the only way to get it back is to squash it. Know what I mean?"

(Cherry)" Actually, a few days ago I 'd have been like what the hell are you talking about? But now I can clearly see where you're coming from. Sometimes you gotta smash some shit to make yourself feel better."

(Keyla)" That is exactly what I mean. So I'm gonna crush that bitch and get my man back."

Cherry's expression changed from joyful to protect your mate. She went straight into jealous woman, you can't talk about my girl like that mode and flipped on Keyla.

(Cherry)" You ain't touching my Stephanie. I won't fucking let you hurt her!" She said as she lunged toward Keyla and nearly knocked her over.

(Keyla)" Hold the hell up? Touching your Stephanie. What the fuck you mean by that? Cherry what's up with that dyke shit?"

Cherry froze where she stood startled by her slip of the tongue and Key's reaction to it. She wondered what to do. Then as quickly as she slipped, she decided to come clean.

(Cherry)" I love her." The young lady said as she looked away in shame.

(Keyla)" You love her? What the fuck are you talking about, you love her? She's a damn chick with a couchie just like you. Ain't you the original dick loving freak? Shit, you love dick more than you love food."

(Cherry)" Stop. Cut it out. This is hard enough as it is, but it's true. I love her and she loves Moe and he loves her and you love him."

(Keyla)" Okay, then why are you so up?"

(Cherry)" Because I did something about it."

(Keyla)" What?
(Cherry)" I kinda told a little white lie that more than likely made a big black man cry."

(Keyla)" Could you stop with all the riddles and just spit it out? What did you tell Moe?"

(Cherry)" I told him about that day when you defended him to Steph when she was first talking about gettin with Slide. I let him know how you sounded like you were feeling him and how Steph wasn't digging him until she saw him with you that day."

(Keyla)" That's the truth any fucking way. That bitch ain't want him until she thought I had him."

(Cherry)" Actually, It is a lie. Stephanie and me were talking that day just before she saw ya'll together and I helped her realize what she was feeling for him. Picture that, I helped the woman I love now see her love for the man she now can't live without. But she really was on her way to confess her love to him. She just had really bad timing."

(Keyla)" So what if it is true. The bitch still don't deserve Moe. But that don't matter right now. What matters now is that your little white lie has given us a chance to flip this to benefit us."

(Cherry)" I know. I didn't really plan on doing it, but the chance came while we were talking so I took it. I felt bad, but I would like to see what her and me could be. And if we can't be anything. I don't want to have to watch her marry him or some shit like that."

(Keyla)" Marry! Oh hell no that shit is not gonna happen while I'm around. Marry that trifling, fake ass don't know a good man when he right under her nose heffa."

(Cherry)" Key, chill okay. I do love the person you are cussing out you know."

(Keyla)" I'm sorry, but I just had to get that out of my system. Okay, just one more thing. She a scank ass hoe with a bad weave. There. Now we need a plan, because you know Moe is extremely understanding and forgiving."

(Cherry)" Yeah, so we have to come up with something."

Break

A Simple Plan

The plan was simple. Cherry would instigate the separation from her end by telling Stephanie that Moe obviously didn't deserve or appreciate her, while Keyla poured on the charm and turned up the heat with Moe. However, simple plans seem to always find a way to complicate themselves and end unexpectedly. Drama likes to attach itself to the simple plan.

(Moe)" Hey, Key."

(Keyla)" Hey."

(Moe)" Can we talk? He asked half heartedly not wanting to upset the pretty woman he'd let down so badly.

(Keyla)" Sure, if you think your girl won't mind."

The comment sounded sarcastic, but it was meant to probe. She wanted to know what the problem was between him and Steph.

(Moe)" That's what I want to talk about. I know you don't really care but I don't want to be in a relationship with her. She's not the person that I thought she was." In his mind he said. " Or hoped she was."

(Keyla)" Oh, so I'm the consolation prize. I win because she lost. What? The pussy wasn't good? She didn't do you like you expected her to?"

(Moe)" Key, I'm not saying that."

(Keyla)" As smart as you are, why can't you understand that actions speak louder than words ever will? First you slept with me, made me your girl, then you slept with her the love of your life, and now you're here again. I'm not the smartest person, but that sorta sounds like the dream fell a little short."

(Moe)" Yeah, it fell short and I set myself up for it. But I got what I deserved. Now I just want to beg you for your forgiveness and hope that we can at least be friends again."

(Keyla)" I don't know 'cause you did hurt me really bad Moe. You were the first guy that I ever let into my heart who didn't have to pay the price of admission. I wanted to give you everything. Even the parts of me I didn't know I had. But you walked away and left me with my legs and my heart wide open. Now, how's a girl supposed to forgive something like that?"

(Moe)" Yeah, you're right. If I were you, I sure as hell wouldn't forgive me either. But that's cool. At least I got to see a part of you that no one else has seen before. And for the record, you are a far more beautiful woman than I ever expected to find under all of that tough girl character you play all of the time."

(Keyla)" See, there you fucking go again being charming and shit trying to break a bitch down with that sweet talk. Like I'm supposed to just open my heart and my legs back up to you after you just been with my former best friend, because you said some of that nice nigga shit. Nope. It don't fucking work like that." Said a pretending to be bitter and angry young woman.

(Moe)" You're right. I'm worse than all of those other guys that hurt you. Damn, all I wanted to do was find out who you are and maybe help you smile more. But all I succeeded in doing was giving you more reason to shield your feelings from the world. I am so sorry, Love. And for what it's worth I never wanted you to stop being my girlfriend. I just got side tracked by the dream."

A very dejected and apologetic Moe turned to leave. But before he could take two steps Keyla interrupted his exit.

(Keyla)" Actually, Moe you did much more than just hurt my heart. Hell, before you I didn't even know I still had one. Let me stop fronting and tell you something. You have been great for me, even if this past week you haven't been nice to me. I mean, before we got together my life was something I can't even really explain. But since, I think about shit, I feel things. Hell, the other day I stopped in a flower shop just to smell the fuckin roses, how corny is that?

(Moe) That's not corny. "That's appreciation."

(Keyla) "I know. But before you all I appreciated was doe and dick. And since you, I really really appreciate dick and the doe part is starting not to matter so much."

(Moe)"Ha,ha. That's real nice of you to say. But why are you telling me this?"

(Keyla) "Because I have never had serious conversations with a man before, I've never needed to call anyone 10x's a day unless it was about money for something. And I've never looked in the mirror before and liked the person looking back at me. I've never said so many full sentences or wished I was in another woman's shoes. I wasn't mad that you lived out your dream. I was just sad that mine was ending so fast." The young ladies eyes began to fill with gum drop sized tears. Her confession wasn't part of the plan, but it would work as if it were.

(Moe) "Love, it's okay. Don't cry, please. I'm so sorry that I put you through this. Stop crying. I don't deserve you . I don't deserve your tears."

(Key)" Baby, no. you deserve everything. You are the best person that I've ever met. You give so much, so easily and with no strings attached. Fuck, so if anyone deserved my love, it's you."

There it was. She had gone and done it. Opened up her chest and served her heart on a platter hot. Hoping that he would take here offering hungrily and savor it like the delicacy it was.

(Moe) "Wow. You really are incredible because that was beautiful. And just so I have this straight, You did just say that you love me, right. I did just hear that?"

(Keyla) "Yeah, I do. More than I know how to."

(Moe) "So, can this horrible, no good man be who he was a week ago?"

(Keyla) "What are you talking about?"

(Moe) "A week ago, I was your boyfriend."

(Keyla) "No. Let's start it fresh and new. You can be my no longer dreaming about Stephanie, because the dream has died, boyfriend. What do you think?"
(Moe) "Yeah, I'd like that."

Although it is a lop-sided idea, some times love starts only on one side of the fence. But even still it has the opportunity to grow just the same. If fate would let them, they would be good together. But unfortunately fate wasn't the only thing that the two love birds had to worry about.

Break

A knock at the door.

(Steph)" Who is it?"

(Cherry)" It's me, Cherry. Open the door."
(Steph)" What do you want? I'm not in the mood to talk right now."

(Cherry)" But it's me. You can always talk to me. So come on, open the door." The young lady pleaded to her friend through the steel barrier.

Steph was reluctant but finally she opened the door and let Cherry in.

(Cherry)" What's wrong with you? Why you tripping like that. Making a chick beg to get in and shit. What's got you all messed up and anti-people?"

Stephanie wasn't really in the mood to deal with Cherry and her lesbian love issues at that particular moment, so she was a little rough on her friend. She spoke to her in a very cold and deliberate manner that caught Cherry a little off guard. However Cherry just brushed it off and blamed it on the whole Moe situation that she had instigated. She never even considered the possibility that Stephanie could care less about her on a romantic level. Cherry had only gone there to find out what had happen between Moe and Steph. She wanted to know where they stood after she had branded her girl a liar in his eyes.

(Steph)" I'm not tripping. I'm just not really feeling the whole company thing right now. I just need some time to work some things out."

(Cherry)" What's up? Last time we talked you were on cloud nine because of your boy. You had just slept with him and it was some bomb-ass sex. So what the hell could mess you up like this after something like that?"

Steph just rolled her eyes and looked at her girl with extreme annoyance. She didn't even attempt to answer her.

(Cherry)" I'm not leaving until you talk to me, girl." She said as she plopped her booty into the love seat.

(Steph)" Damn! You're a stubborn bitch ain't you? Fine. If your nosy ass must know, Moe told me that we can't be together. Okay? Your nosy ass happy now?"

(Cherry)" Of course I'm not happy. Baby, you okay?

(Steph)" No I'm not okay and I ain't your baby. So don't fucking call me that."

(Cherry)" But?"

(Steph)" But nothing. I ain't your girlfriend and

this ain't no I love you relationship. I'm supposed to be his girlfriend."

A stunned Cherry burst into uncontrollable tears and almost violent convulsions, as her brain tried to make sense of what the woman she loved was saying to her. It could not be possible that her friend and recent love interest had been using her the whole time.

(Cherry)" But what about us?" The young woman murmured already knowing the answer.

(Steph)" Us? What the fuck you mean us? I licked your pussy and you licked mine, so what. It ain't mean shit but an orgasm."

(Cherry)" That's it? That's all it was to you was a fucking nut. But I fucking love you. I'm not even sure that I'm gay but I know how I feel about you."

(Steph)" Well then you gotta figure that shit out for yourself, without my help. Because I ain't no homosexual and I sure don't love no chick, when it's so much dick in the world."

(Cherry)" Then why the fuck were you combing my hair, kissing me so sweet and telling me that you would never hurt me like them niggas did, if you wasn't feeling me like that. You supposed to be my girl, my motherfucking friend and shit. Why would you lead me on like that and then hurt me like this? What did I do to you to deserve this?"

(Steph)" I never meant to hurt you. I just needed to make sure that you'd be on my side in my fight against Key for Moe's heart. Being with him is all I care about."

(Cherry)" So all I was... No, all I am is a tool in your quest for the perfect fucking man. A man that doesn't even trust you anymore."

(Steph)" Hold up. What made you say that?"

Cherry hesitated, but her anger loosened her tongue causing something very big to take place. All of a sudden she revealed her part in Moe's leaving.

(Cherry)" You used me to get your dream. Well I stole your dream, bitch."

(Steph)" What the fuck is your crazy ass talking about?"

(Cherry)" Yeah, I,m crazy. Crazy enough to tell your boy Moe that you didn't want him until you saw him with Keyla."

(Steph)" What! Bitch, I'm gonna..."

Break

Slide had been hiding out in the vacant apartment on the top floor of Stephanie's building since he found out that there was a warrant out for his arrest. Steph had pressed charges after he had attacked her on that dark street near the theater. He couldn't believe the bitch had done it, especially since she had gotten the better of him. So now he was a fugitive, but even worse than that he was a street corner pharmacist who couldn't apply his trade because of a snitching ass bitch with a big booty. He had been biding his time and waiting for the perfect opportunity to strike. The chance to beat her face in with his initial ring until those very initials were a permanent part of her cheek.

Slide had been watching her since shortly after their last encounter. Hiding in the shadows, peeping around corners, even following her home every single day, until he had learned her every move. He knew about the Cherry situation, her beef with Keyla and wished he had a sniper rifle every time that he saw that goody-goody Moe nigga. But he was a hustler, so he had patience. The brother understood that if he played his game right and waited long enough, Steph would forget about him and a legitimate chance for revenge would present itself. And here it was, that perfect moment he'd been waiting for all of this time. While he waited on the stairs and watched cherry go into the apartment, Slide noticed that there were no three clicks after the door had closed. Every single day he heard the three distinct clicking sounds of the locks on Stephanie's door. Deadbolt locks that prevented him from sneaking in while she slept and ripping her snitching pink tongue from her mouth by the root. Yanking it brutally and bloodily from between her perfect lips with dirty grease covered pliars. After which he would fuck her in that fat ass one last time before she bled to death. In his mind, he knew that the plan sounded insane, but to him that was the kind of thing that a snitching ass bitch deserved. And if he had it in him, that's what she'd get.

Break

Cherry quickly jumped to her feet as Stephanie rushed toward her with hate in her eyes. Cherry's level of aggression was just as high as her friends. The two women grabbed at each others hair, scratched at each others eyes, pulled on each others clothes and threw heavy punches that sounded like thunder clapping in the distance when they connected with flesh.

So, this is what love looks like when it's misused and misinterpreted? Two dear friend's for so many years, all of a sudden at each others throats, tearing at each others clothes, pulling at hair, scratching at eyes and trying to draw blood. One of them, in her own twisted way fighting for love while the other quickly approaches that thin line that keeps hate at bay. Both women had crossed that line and become just a little Love Crazy. Placed in a state of frenzy by an emotion that they've only caught a glimpse of, never really thought they needed or wanted and can't quite get a handle on.

Break

The young ladies were so bent on getting at each others throats, that they never even noticed Slide slip into the room. He stood there silently for a moment watching the women express there aggression until finally Cherry froze and stopped throwing punches. Stephanie was about to deliver a heavy blow to Cherry's undefended cheek when her eyes peered over her friends shoulder and finally spotted the gun toting felon. There he was leaning defiantly against the door, with his freshly polished firearm pointing in the girls' general direction.

(Slide)" Hey, don't stop on my account. I love a good chick fight."

(Cherry)" Slide, what are you doing here and why you got a gun?"

(Slide)" Shut up, bitch. I ain't here for you. I'm here for her. The snitching ass hoe who got the fucking cops chasing after me."

(Steph)" What the fuck you want with me? You ain't get enough the last time I saw you?" She said with blatant defiance and obvious sarcasm.

(Slide)" Oh, so you a tough chick now? Alright let's see just how tough you really are bitch." He said as he rushed her and hit her in the cheek with the butt of his shiny new gun knocking her to the floor.

Cherry jumped at him, but her attempt at heroics was interrupted by the impact of metal across her face also. The blood splattered everywhere staining curtains and floors. The two young women huddled together in a sobbing mass, while their assailant hovered over them. He gloated like their pain was fueling his ego. His smile was unsettling and coupled with the sound of a round sliding into the chamber sent chills through both young ladies. Even though Stephanie had sworn to never be afraid of him again, the fear coursed through her veins. Slide looked like a man possessed. It was like the gun was re-establishing his heart and making him brave enough to do the things that he had considered earlier.

(Slide)" Yeah, look at you now. Where all your brave shit at now bitch? I don't hear you talking any more. Maybe if I stick this gun in your mouth it will give you something to say."

(Cherry)" Please don't hurt her."

(Slide)" Didn't I tell you this ain't about you? Didn't you hear me with your dumb dyke ass?" Slide said as he leaned down and waved the 9 millimeter in Cherries face. Not so gently tapping it against her cheek.

(Slide)" Don't you understand that she don't feel shit for you? She don't feel shit for nobody but that Moe motherfucka. If anything, you were just something to do or just a quick tongue lick. You one of them pretty dumb bitches ain't you? Okay, so let me spell it out for you. She don't love nobody but that big broke nigga Moe that's fucking both ya'll best friend Keyla and maybe that little noisy ass rug rat of hers."

Cherry wanted to curse him out, but the gun waving from side to side deterred her and dulled her usually sharp tongue. Stephanie held back too, because it was really dark down the barrel of that death bringing weapon that Slide was holding so nonchalantly.

(Steph)" What Slide? What do you want from me? What do you want me to do?"

(Slide)" Now that's more like it. Calm your ass down and talk real nice to the nigga with the gun. That's how it's supposed to be. But I'll get to you in a minute. I want some of your girl's attention first. I've had you, but I haven't had any of little Miss sweet as Cherry pie over here and word on the streets is that she a for real freak." Slide said as he rubbed the gun against his manhood.

With his gun in hand, Slide felt like he was in total control of the situation, so he let his anger at Stephanie subside just a little and diverted his attention to his perverse nature. Fundamentally, the young man was a pervert at heart with a need to control women. And at that particular moment, Cherry was in his sights and he was dieing to shoot her in the face. However, the plan was not to use his gun.

(Steph)" You just a fucking pervert and a punk. Gotta use a gun to get pussy. You just fucking pathetic." Stephanie's courage began to rise again as she verbally assaulted Slide in defense of her friend.

Slide spun in her direction with violent force and smacked her across the face with the back of his hand. But Stephanie's courage continued to grow even with the blood flowing from her mouth. She had returned to that place within herself where Slide and men like him had no more power over her. She struggled to her feet and continued to call him every derogatory name that came to mind. Cherry tried to stop her and calm her down.

(Cherry)" Steph, stop it! Stop it please. It's okay. I'll do whatever he wants if it will keep him from pulling that trigger. Calm down please."

(Steph)" No. Fuck that nigga! He want to shoot me, then he better go the fuck ahead and shoot me. I ain't never gonna let him hurt me again or anybody that I care about while I'm around."

Cherry was touched by the fact that her friend would defend her even if it meant her life. They may not have been meant to be lovers, but it was obvious to Cherry at that moment, that they really had been friends all of these years. Then like a bomb exploding unexpectedly, Slide pointed the gun at the wall and pulled the trigger. The bullet barely missed Stephanie's rib cage before it went into the wall. The two women were again frozen by that same uncontrollable fear that had gripped them a short time earlier.

(Slide)" Ya'll finished. Understand that I am not playing and I will shoot both you bitches. Especially you with your tougher than any nigga attitude problem." Slide screamed as he pointed the gun in Steph's face.

Stephanie was breathing hard and trying to concentrate through her fear of being shot. It was working at first but all of a sudden she realized that Joy was crying. Then the reality of the situation smacked her upside of her head almost as hard as Slide had hit her with the gun. The reality that if she did not relax and calm down, this sick ass, pretty faced maniac with the nice ride would pull the trigger of his 9 and kill her leaving Joy without a mother or a father. As much as she hated him, she couldn't risk doing that to her baby.

(Steph)" Alright. You win. Whatever you want, but just hurry up and get it over with."

(Cherry)" Yeah. We won't fight you. Just tell us

what you want us to do and we'll do it. Just don't hurt us."

Slide's grin stretched from ear to ear, as he began to think of exactly what he wanted them to do for him and to each other. At that moment he felt like the most powerful man in the whole wide world.
(Slide)" Kiss each other." He said with wide-eyed enthusiasm.

The two young ladies gave each other a half-hearted nervous kiss that Slide interrupted with an angry outburst.

(Slide)" No! Fucking kiss like you would your man. I want tongue and I want to see some spit-swapping. Some shit that'll make my dick get hard. None of that bullshit ya'll just did."

They hesitated, but eventually their tongues found each other and Slide's gun found the hardness of his crotch again. Their exchange turned him on just like he knew it would. And on the other end of it, Cherry's excitement grew too. Her heart raced almost too fast for her to keep it in her chest at the anticipation of kissing Stephanie again. Slide was helping her be close to her girl again and she was going to take full advantage of the situation. But for Stephanie it was different. Her heart was beating like the drums of those ancient tribesmen who used the rhythm to fuel their fire. And her anger grew like anger has the tendency to do when it has to hide itself.

(Slide)" Now let me see them fat asses. Stand up, turn around and take those tight damn jeans off. Do that shit slow too."

The two women rose, turned around and slowly removed their overly tight jeans. And then there they stood exposing bottoms that any man would gladly pay to see. Slide had to sit down because his excitement was growing and his erection was stealing all of the blood from his brain. He sat in the chair, unzipped his pants and watched the show that he was in complete control of.

(Slide)" I can't take this shit no more, Cherry come here."

Slide grabbed her by her wrists and pulled her down to her knees in front of him, while forcefully grabbing the back of her neck with his gun hand. She gagged and tried to gather herself, but the butt of the gun was driving into her neck and his dick was nearing the back of her throat, choking her.

(Steph)" Cut it out. Can't you see you're choking her?"

Slide barely acknowledge Stephanie, however he did loosen his grip slightly. Just enough so that Cherry could breathe, but not enough to let himself out of her mouth.

(Slide)" Suck that dick you little bitch. Suck my dick."

It was Slide saying the words but Cherry could swear that she was hearing the sound of her father's voice. Screaming in her ears to suck his dick and forcing himself repeatedly into her mouth. She started to tremble and shake. Memories that just seemed all wrong flooded her mind. None of that had actually happened to her, or did it? The feelings were overwhelming her senses and she began to feel trapped and afraid. Like a little girl locked in a closet because she didn't do what she was told. Her panic started to show on her face and she started to move around violently fighting to get free of Slide's grip. He would not let her go until her teeth began to grind against the flesh of his manhood. He screamed, pushed her to the floor, jumped up and shoved the gun in her face.

(Slide)" Bitch! What the fuck are you doing? That's not how the fuck you suck a Dick. You don't fucking bite it like that. I should shoot your dumb ass. Biting my damn dick like that."

Slide hit Cherry forcefully against her cheek with his gun hand causing her to fall out flat on the floor in tears. However, in her mind Slide wasn't hitting her. She could still hear her father's voice and every single time that his hand struck her face, the young distraught woman could see her father's image grow clearer. And deep within herself she could feel the fears of a 9 year old girl growing and overcoming her heart. The anxiety curled her up into a tight little ball in the middle of the floor and then a knock at door interrupted the scene.

(Slide)" Shut up! None of ya'll bitches bet not say shit."

He quietly approached the door and peeked through the peephole. For a second his heart stopped and his breathing was staggered by the sudden lump in his throat. It was Moe and Keyla on the other side of the door. Slide's true bitch nature started to rear its head until he remembered that there was a gun in his hand. Then his fear shifted to nervous excitement at the prospect of pistol whipping that punk nigga Moe who had embarrassed him in front of his boys. And being the pervert that he is, the idea of having Keyla there too meant that he would get to exploit all three of the women who had been on his mind. He raised the gun and quickly opened the door.

(Slide)" Come in. Won't the two of you join the party." He said as he pointed the gun directly in Moe's unsuspecting face.

(Moe)" What the fuck?"

(Keyla)" Oh shit!"

(Slide)" You bet not fucking run either or I'm a shoot both ya'll sorry asses."

Stephanie had taken the opportunity to put her pants back on and pick up her keys from the table, while Slide was preoccupied.

(Slide)" Get the fuck in here before somebody see ya'll. Damn I must have done some really good shit in a past life or some shit to be this fucking lucky. Now I got the whole motherfucking gang all together in one place at the same time. I am gonna enjoy this shit here."

Slide was as excited as he'd ever been in his life, at the prospect of having the chance to deal with everyone who had any part at all in the disruption of his former Ghetto Superstardom. He ushered Moe and Keyla into the apartment where they saw their two battered and bruised friends. Slide pushed Key over to where the other two women were and then grabbed Moe by the back of his shirt and shoved the gun behind his ear. Moe's fear showed in his eyes and was evident by the sweat on his brow. Every bead of perspiration fueled Slide's courage. It was a courage harbored in the barrel of a gun and waiting for an excuse to release its aggression.

(Keyla)" Why are you doing this? This shit is crazy. "

(Slide)" Oh, so I'm crazy. Nah, what's crazy is your wanna be tough ass talking shit to a man with a loaded gun."

He said while switching the direction of his gun barrel towards her. The young lady could see the signs of an unfamiliar resolve behind his eyes. Slide wasn't flipping out and being emotional, it kind of looked like he was getting off on the situation and that realization scared the shit out of the usually hard to shake Keyla.

(Slide)" Now what you need to do is shut the fuck up and hope that I don't shoot your too tough acting ass in your always open mouth."

(Moe)" Slide there's no need to get upset. Nobody needs to get hurt."

Slide smacked Moe in the back of the head with the gun barrel knocking him to the floor.

(Slide)" Now you know you need to shut the hell up! 'Cause you are definitely not leaving here without some holes in your ass. Fucking always trying to save the world and thinking that you are some kind of Super Nigga or some shit. Nigga you ain't bullet proof and if you don't shut the hell up, we are all about to find out right now."

(Steph)" Slide why are you paying attention to them? We were in the middle of something weren't we?"

Stephanie wanted to draw Slide's attention back to her and Cherry, since he really didn't want to kill them. It was about sex with them. But she knew that if he kept his mind on Moe eventually the courage to pull the trigger would build and Moe was her heart, so she couldn't let anything happen to him. Then all of a sudden a great idea popped into her head.

(Steph)" You should sit that sorry cheating on his girl-ass nigga down over there and make him watch you fuck his girl."

(Keyla)" Bitch! How you gonna give my pussy away?"

(Steph)" What's the difference? You give the shit away like it's government cheese anyway bitch."

(Slide)" I told ya'll to shut the fuck up. And besides, shooting his girl in the mouth with my dick, with him watching would definitely feel better than shooting that nigga in the head. And since you are his girl and don't want to see him dead and all, I'm sure you won't mind showing me some affection" Slide said as he slid his hand across Keyla's ass.

No one seemed to notice that Cherry was staring off into space and mumbling as if she were talking to someone invisible. They didn't see the anxiety welling up in her face or notice that she was not in the same room that they were in at that moment. She was someplace very far away. Slide's brutality and aggression had created a situation of powerlessness for Cherry and made her regress. It reminded her of something.

Break

Cherry was locked in a moment that she had long ago forgotten. In a place where a 9 year old girl, who had developed too soon, was at the mercy of people who wanted to use her for the satisfaction of their own selfish needs.

(Cherry)" Momma! Momma! Don't make me. Please don't let him make me do this."

(Lorna)" Baby it's okay. They just want to look at what a big girl you are, so don't be a baby. Just take the damn dress off. Ain't nobody gonna hurt you while yo momma and daddy here. Your daddy just want to show his friends how proud he is of his baby. So take off the damn dress before I slap the taste out your mouth."

Cherry was stunned by her mother's words. Her young ears couldn't believe what they were hearing. So she hesitated because the words had to be wrong. Her mother would never tell her to get undressed in front of a room filled with men that included her father.

(Cherry)" Momma, no. I can't get undressed in front of..."

The slap was loud and it resonated through the room filled with drunk and high on more than life adults. Cherry sobbed heavily as she removed her little nightdress and watched the eyes of every man in the place slide over her form with eager perversion. She used to feel special being the only child at the grown up parties, but now all she felt was afraid, ashamed and in danger.

(Lorna)" Look at her. I ain't get titties like that until I was almost 16. The damn girl is barely 10 and got a body like a damn whore already."

(Lorna's Daddy)" You shut your mouth. Don't call my angel no damn whore. That's my baby. Come here baby and sit on your daddy's lap. I won't let nobody hurt you girl."

She walked slowly across the room towards her father who never once looked her in her eyes. Every man in the room was either licking his lips or rubbing his crotch. The alcohol and drugs had released all of their demons and at that moment every hellish abomination in the room was hoping that the young supple virgin would be sacrificed before the night was over.

Break

(Moe)" You going to have to shoot me, because I won't let you hurt any one of these women while I'm here."

Moe was scared out of his mind, but his manhood would not let Slide degrade or abuse any of his friends in his presence. He wouldn't have been able to live with himself if he did.

(Slide)" Damn! You just never stop. Do you? What the fuck? You wanna be some kind of superhero or some shit?"

(Moe)" Naw, I'm no hero."

(Slide)" I know you ain't no fucking hero. Heroes don't go around fucking best friends and ruining friendships that have been around longer than he has. Heroes don't swear they love a bitch one day and then run up in they best friend the next. I read comic books motherfucker and superman ain't never do no shit like that."

(Steph)" That's the first smart thing I ever heard you say."

Moe was caught off guard by Slide's humorous and very true statement. He was sure that no one in the room believed him to be a superhero anymore, but he would risk his life for them in this instant whether they had faith in his sincerity or not. Stephanie saw her opportunity

224 · Sean M. Cleveland

to regain some semblance of control and ran with it.

(Steph)" Yeah, first you blast me for not telling you how I feel and then for having a boyfriend. Then you fight my boyfriend and ask me to leave him, but when I say no, you go and fuck one of my best friends to get back at me. Then you flaunt it right in my face to make me jealous and when that works and I start feeling you, you tell me how deeply you love me and then fuck my brains out. Giving me the impression that we gonna have a relationship or some shit and live happily ever after, but then you leave my bed before I even wake the fuck up and run back to your girl who you don't want to hurt, even though you don't love the bitch. Yeah, you're right. You ain't no fucking hero. Hell after what you've done to me and Keyla, I don't even know if you're a nice fucking guy or just like every other nigga. So don't defend my honor from him, somebody should be defending us from you."

(Keyla)" Bitch, you need to slow you role. Moe has been nothing but good to you for years and you played with his heart every chance that you got. So don't stand over there acting all holier than fucking thou and shit."

(Steph)" You just a dumb bitch caught up on some good fucking dick. This nigga called you his girl and then fucked me like you didn't even exist."

Stephanie had struck a cord in both Keyla and Moe. Moe was silent and Key's anger was growing and growing. Her plan had begun to work.

(Keyla)" Yeah, he fucked up and made a mistake, but I can forgive his one mistake when he's standing here defending me with his life. Now you're dumb ass is talking shit when he's trying to defend your life too? Hell, he's defended you for as long as he's known you and because you can't be his girl, you want to condemn him for giving in to his needs. And then worse of all you want to side with the nigga that beat your ass and got the fucking gun pointed at all of us. Yeah, you a piece of fucking work alright and somebody needs to beat yo dumb jealous ass."

(Steph)" You sure ain't the bitch to do it. I know that shit."

(Slide)" You two are some funny mother fuckers. I'm standing here with the gun and ya'll arguing over who gets to be this asshole's bitch. Well, I'm sick of it. So shut the fuck up."

(Steph)" I'm gonna shut up but you should still fuck that bitch and make him watch. Disrespect him like he been disrespecting you this whole time."

Stephanie knew that she was risking everything with her plan to focus Slide's attention on

Keyla. She understood that Moe might defend his girl, but she hoped that her long time girlfriend's temper would reach its boiling point first. That way Slide would be given reason to shoot Keyla before attempting to hurt anyone else. Or at the least he'd let her finally get her fists on Keyla. Either way the commotion would allow someone to get the gun away from Slide's crazy ass.

Slide was not as dumb as Stephanie hoped that he was, because he recognized that she was trying to lead his attention away from Moe. However at that particular moment there was too much ass in the room for Slide to think straight. Even if it was part of a plan, he thought that fucking Keyla's pretty ass was a damn good idea.

(Slide)" Everybody over there by Cherry. I need a minute to think this through."

They moved to where he directed them and stood waiting for his next order. Moe stood next to Stephanie and Keyla stood close by Cherry who was still on the floor in her under wear. Stephanie rubbed against Moe and dropped her keys into his pocket while Slide wasn't looking. At that moment he understood why she had said all of those mean things a minute ago. Then he acted as if he were going to pass out and Keyla grabbed him to keep him from falling.

(Moe)" Keyla act like you are giving in to him and distract him toward to window."

She didn't understand, but she trusted her man enough to do what he had asked her to.

(Keyla)" Fuck it. If it will get us out of here lets just do this shit." Keyla said as she removed her shirt and walked toward the window unbuckling her belt.

(Slide)" See, now that's what I'm talking about. Cooperate and help a brother out. Then this whole situation might not end up so messy."

Slide walked over to keyla and squeezed her breasts. She moaned which excited him causing him to turn his attention away from Moe and Stephanie. At that moment Moe turned quickly and threw the keys in Slide's face catching him off guard and causing him to drop the gun. Keyla pushed Slide over the chair and kicked the gun away while Moe and Stephanie rushed Slide. Their captor scrambled and started swinging wildly. His terror rose as his courage faded. All he wanted to do was get his gun back or get to the fire escape. The gun was on the floor next to Cherry and in order to get to it he would have to get passed Moe, Steph and Keyla, so instead he ran for the window. Moe climbed out the window after him and chased him down the fire escape. The women rushed to the window but didn't follow. They just watched the chase. On the other side of the room, Cherry picked up the gun and began to scream out of control.

(Cherry)" Daddy! Daddy, no! Please don't. Please don't make me do that. I can't do that. Momma, help me! Somebody help me."

She was distraught, afraid, angry and frantic. Her hands trembled as she pointed the gun in every direction as if aiming at invisible assailants. The young woman was huffing, puffing and moving around hap hazard like she was trying to keep people from touching her. Stephanie and Cherry turned to see what was wrong with their friend and were stunned by what they witnessed. Cherry bumped into things, stumbled, spun around, pointed and waved the gun in every direction. She was trapped in her memory and unable to find her way back.

(Keyla)" Cherry. What's the matter girl? Come on put the gun down,"

(Steph)" Yeah. Give me the gun girl. Your momma and daddy ain't here."

The two women realized that their girl had broken down and that they had a very big problem. Cherry was having a nervous breakdown or something like that and had a gun in her hand. A gun that could go off at any minute and hurt or kill any one of them.

(Steph)" Key, we gotta get that gun out of her hand."

(Keyla)" How do we do that? She over there talking to people that I sure as hell can't see, but she obviously can. And if we get too close she might get confused and shoot one of us."

(Steph)" I'll do it, since you're scared. Besides she wouldn't hurt me anyway."

Stephanie was relying heavily on the fact that Cherry was in love with her to ensure her safety. She felt that if Cherry could hear her voice and recognize her everything would be okay. This was a huge gamble, since at that moment in time her friend wasn't even in the same room as her. She was still in a place where her fear was her only protection; at least it was until she picked up that gun.

(Steph)" Baby, It's me. It's me Stephanie. Can you hear me? Cherry it's okay. Nobody is gonna hurt you. I will protect you."

Strangely enough, Cherry could actually hear Stephanie's voice. It sounded like it was off in the distance, but she did hear it. Her movement s began to slow and calm. The young lady lowered the gun and stood silent for a long moment. Cherry almost looked bewildered and lost. That's probably how she felt just then. Like a child separated from her innocence for the first time with no one to explain it to her and help her through it. She could hear Stephanie talking to her at a distance, but still felt the presence of strangers who wanted to hurt her.

(Cherry)" Stephanie? Where are you? Can you help me? They are going to hurt me. Please don't let them hurt me."

(Steph)" I won't let anyone hurt you. You know that. I am here for you. Just listen to my voice and calm down."
(Cherry)" Please hurry. They are getting closer to me and I am scared. Don't let them do this to me, please."

Stephanie's efforts to ease Cherry's mood were working. The young lady was standing stationary and no longer waving the gun around. Then Stephanie began to walk slowly towards her friend.

(Steph)" Come on Baby hand me the gun. It's okay. Everything is going to be fine. I will protect you from all of those bad people, because I love you."

(Cherry)" You love me? You don't fucking love me!. You love that nigga Moe. You just used me to help you get to him. You don't fucking love me!"

Cherry's anger brought her back to the reality of her situation; the fact that her best friend had seduced her and stolen her heart just so that she could use it later if she needed to. Cherry's heart pumped furiously in her chest as she stood there in her pretty pink panties holding Slide's gun. She had escaped the memories that were holding on to her so tightly, however the pain and powerlessness escaped with her. They intermingled with her anger and created a rage that Stephanie was standing directly in front of.

(Steph)" Calm down, Cherry. It's okay."

(Cherry)" No it's not okay. You hurt me bad. You just used me like everybody else who was supposed to love me did. You never fucking loved me."
Her love for Stephanie was so big that it held the anger back like a dam. However, her hatred of her parents and herself fueled her hostility and unfortunately Stephanie was in it's path.

(Keyla)" Cherry. Cherry! It's okay girl. Now I have never hurt you and I never would. So listen to me and just let it go."

(Cherry)" What are you talking about? Let it go? How the fuck do I just let it go? I can't take it any more! I am not a doormat, I'm not trash and I am not a piece of shit! I matter!. I mean something." Said the young lady as angry tears welled up in her eyes again.

(Keyla)" I know, Cherry. You are a wonderful person and a lot of people have hurt you. But don't let them win. You are better than they are."

Stephanie stood there with a look of fear on her face tempered with a hint of disdain. Cherry could see this clearly and it enraged her further. She put her other hand on the gun and shook slightly.

(Cherry)" Look at that bitch face. Look at her face. Looking at me like I ain't worth shit. I told her my secrets and she used them to get a man. To get a fucking man that doesn't even fucking want her anymore. Ain't that fucked up. The bitch ain't even sorry that she hurt me and we been friends forever."

(Steph)" I am sorry. Sorry that I hurt you, my dear friend. Sorry that I hurt your heart for my own selfish reasons. I am really sorry for all of that. But the time we shared together was special to me too. It's just the whole Moe and Keyla thing had me crazy. I just can't even explain it."

Stephanie's apology was masterful. It was swaying Cherry back to her side again. Cherry could relate to the notion that what Stephanie felt for Moe had clouded her judgment and caused her to hurt her friend.

(Cherry)" Yeah. Yeah. Love is crazy sometimes

and it can definitely make a person do crazy things. Maybe. Maybe, you didn't mean to hurt me like you did. But why are you looking at me like that. Like I disgust you."

(Steph)" I'm just scared. Scared that I'll get shot. Scared that Joy will have no mother to raise her. Scared that my best friend hates me enough to kill me, because I hurt her so bad."

Stephanie was doing it again. She was taking advantage of Cherry's vulnerability. However, this time it was in an effort to save her skin.

(Steph)" Cherry. You have always been like a sister to me, so this whole situation just freaked me out a little bit. I didn't know how to deal with it, so I handled it in the worst possible way. I treated something beautiful like it was dirty, like it didn't matter when it mattered so much. I just don't know what to do."

At that moment Stephanie was glad that she had spent so much time with Moe and paid such close attention to him when he spoke. Because at that moment when she needed words most, his words came in handy.

(Steph)" Cherry listen to me. No matter what you feel right now, just take a minute and think about what you're about to do. You are about to shoot one of your best friends and probably kill her. There is no taking that back. If you pull the trigger I will be gone forever. Is that what you really want?"

(Cherry)" No. I don't want you to be gone forever. I would miss you so much. I love you."

Cherry's muscles began to relax and her hands slowly lowered along with the gun. Her anger had subsided. She felt like herself again. Her tears flowed heavily as the pain emptied from her heart. The young lady hurt so bad just then and probably would for a long time to come.

(Steph)" Come here. It's okay. We can figure something out. We both need a hand with this love stuff."

Moe walked in just as Stephanie embraced Cherry tenderly. Since he had not witnessed the exchange, there was a baffled look on his face.

(Moe)' What's going on?"

His timing and Stephanie's reaction could not have been worse. When he walked in, Keyla's eyes got big and she rushed to him. Then Stephanie pushes Cherry to the side and started to rush in Moe's direction too. And before she realized the significance of her response, a shot rang out echoing through the room. Time froze in dramatic fashion while the bullet searched out its target and found refuge in the flesh of its victim.

His breathing became erratic as the burning sensation shot through his chest. Moe's blood flowed like a red river saturating dirty tiles as his body crumbled to the floor. The room filled with the screams of distraught women who could not believe what they had just witnessed.

(Keyla)" Moe! Moe! Baby, no! Please baby, no!" She said as she dropped to her knees beside the only man she'd ever had any real feelings for in her life.

Stephanie turned toward Cherry with hate in her eyes and a hostile heart. She breathed heavily and walked slowly toward the woman who had just shot down the love of her life. The young lady never even considered the idea that the gun was still loaded and still in the hands of an unstable person whose heart she had broken.

(Cherry)" Stop! Don't make me shoot you! I don't want to shoot you."
(Steph)" What the fuck did you do? You shot him. You fucking shot him?"

(Cherry)" Yeah, I shot him. I didn't want to shoot him. But he is the reason you don't love me. He's the reason you hurt me so bad. That's what you said. You pushed me to the side for him. How could you do that?"

Cherry was slipping back into that place where

all her hurt resided. That place where sunlight couldn't reach and hope didn't exist. She was lost and feeling betrayed again. Stephanie's distress about Moe being shot had washed away all of her pretenses in regard to loving Cherry. She had taken an aggressive stance and there was so much hate in her eyes. Cherry saw it clearly and prepared to respond accordingly.

And there they were standing face to face locked in a moment that only one of them could walk away from. Cherry consumed in gloom and bitterness pointing a gun at her friend whose love and heart she craved. Stephanie boiling with the rage of lose and despair since the man of her dreams was lying on the floor bleeding to death.

(Cherry)" You better stop! Don't come any closer. I really don't want to hurt you. Please don't make me hurt you. Please."

(Steph)" You might as well fucking shoot me too. The man I love is over there on the floor dying, because of your crazy ass, so you might as well shoot me too."

(Cherry)" Shut up! I didn't mean to shoot Moe. He's a nice guy. I didn't mean to hurt him and I am not crazy! I'm just upset right now and a little confused."

(Steph)" Confused? Confused people don't

shoot people for no good God-Damn reason."

(Cherry)" No reason? I have every reason to want him out of the picture. Maybe not to kill him, but definitely to want him out of the picture. He kept you from me. You just said so yourself a minute ago, that what you feel for him messed up your head when it came to dealing with what we feel."

(Steph)" Bitch there is no us. I ain't fucking confused about shit. I love him and only him. Is that clear enough. So all you've done is make me hate you and sent your ass to fucking prison or the damn crazy house."

Cherry knew that every word Stephanie was speaking was true this time, because she could feel the disgust in her friend's words. Just then she realized that none of her ideas about her and Stephanie were even remotely possible. All of their time together had been false. Stephanie could care less about her feelings and what she wanted. All Steph wanted was Moe. And on top of all of that, she had just shot Moe. A guy that she really liked and kind of admired over someone who could care less about her. There he was on the floor of Stephanie's apartment, gasping for air while the ambulance rushed to help him. There he was laying in a pool of blood that seemed to be growing at a very rapid rate, while Keyla clung to him and Stephanie badgered Cherry.

The young gun wielding woman's body began to grow still, as the movie of her life replayed itself in her mind. She watched quietly as pigtailed dreams turned into pony-tailed nightmares that left a bitter taste in her mouth. She could see their faces, she could hear their voices and she could still smell the stale scent of alcohol on their breaths as tears formed in the corners of her eyes. She felt the shame that came with the unwanted pleasure and then the touch of fingers that made her stomach turn and convulse. She felt the cold of loneliness that held her secretly for so long and then finally the pain of lose. Cherry had lost a huge portion of herself a long time ago, somewhere among the wreckage of her childhood and today with the squeeze of a trigger she had given away the remainder of herself.

As Stephanie turned to check on Moe, the gun rose, the trigger squeezed, the bullet enter the flesh of an unsuspecting back, Keyla screamed and then a long silence filled the room. A silence that was shattered by the heartfelt apologizes of a young woman about to hopefully set herself free from an existence that she could no longer take.

(Cherry)" I'm sorry Keyla. I never meant to hurt you or Moe. I am so very sorry. And I am sorry that I ever believed a word that you said Stephanie, you fucking lying bitch. But more than anything, I'm sorry for not being a better person or worth loving."

So as she watched the blood flow from the back of the woman she loved, Cherry raised the gun, told Keyla that she was sorry again, said goodbye to Stephanie and then pulled the trigger one last time sending a bullet through her mouth and then out the back of her head. Moe's life was in jeopardy, Stephanie's life was in question, Keyla's life would never be the same and Cherry's life was over because love had done what it often does when handled improperly by those people fortunate enough to find it. It destroyed them.

Conclusion

We as individuals in need of connection tend to look to love as our salvation. We place far too many expectations on it. Love is supposed to solve all of our problems, erase heart ache, help us forget and help us rebuild. Actually most times we as human beings demand these things from Love, when all love promises us is an opportunity. A chance to feel something worthwhile and tangible. Sure it can do all of the things that we expect of it if we embrace it openly and treat it with respect. Unfortunately we seldom handle Love properly. And then when Love leaves or dies, we blame Love for it all.

The Love wasn't strong enough. The Love wasn't real or it wasn't true. Then we harden our hearts to it and hold a grudge, which fundamentally hinders our ability to legitimately love again. And what is crazy to this writer is that all Love is, is a feeling. A very powerful and compelling feeling, but just a feeling none the less. An emotion that offers you everything, but promises you nothing. Love has no expectations of us. And as a result of our not understanding the true nature of Love and all of its subtle nuances and intricacies, our lives begin to resemble Greek tragedies. Relationships turn into epic adventures or Odysseys that tell tales of tragic heroes who become monsters, miss out on the point of life, value the wrong things and suffer cruel unimaginable fates.

The story of Moe, Keyla, Stephanie, Slide and Cherry is a clear example of an Urban Greek Tragedy in relation to not understanding the dynamics of Love. The idea that some loves shouldn't last and need to be let go of. Even when they are true and deserving loves, sometimes because of circumstance or just because of the timing they should not be held on to. Some loves are one sided and are doomed from the start, because only one person feels it. It's a lopsided love that can cause serious problems, so it should be let go of. And then there is the fact that all loves to some degree are possessive leading to those experiences that cross the line into the obsessive, the controlling and the out of control. Turning the idea of Love into an abusive situation that should be let go of. And sadly there are a great many loves that are tainted by their own misinterpretation. Meaning that some loves have no respect in them, some loves have no understanding in them and some loves anticipate more than they should.

We as people are flawed by design and as a result so are most of the Loves that we attempt to share with one another. And unfortunately a lot of the time we feel a Love that should not last or that can't sustain itself under the pressures of the lives we've chosen to live. But because it is Love we stay connected and hold on to it with all of our might, even when it hurts physically, even when it undermines our character and even when it no longer looks like Love. And it will remain an unfortunate circumstance until the day we as creatures of emotion who are brave enough to be vulnerable, smart enough to recognize it at first glance and tough enough to work at it, learn that sometimes even with Love; You have to Let it Go.

Dedication Page

This book would never have come to be if it were not for those people in my life who displayed more belief in my ability than even I had myself. Those few select individuals who constantly asked me if I was still working on it, repeatedly asked if they could help in any way, maybe by reading it or just listening to my thoughts on what direction to take it in. Without their support and wholehearted belief in my ability to do this whole book thing, this entire experience would still be just a fantasy wished for and not the dream it is, that I am living. For that I love you guys and dedicate this book to all of you Beautiful people that got me to this point.

Without your friendship and genuine, unwavering faith, I would have probably Let It

Go and just stopped like so many people do. But through it all, you guys who are very important to me got past the doubts and helped me to realize that since I love to write I should even if no one else appreciates it. I should do it for me because I want to and it is what I enjoy so much. I would say your names, but I know you guys so well and can here you saying that you do not need the recognition or want the attention. You would tell me that as long as I know who you are and what you did for me, that's enough. So again I say thank you again from the bottom of my heart and the edge of my soul.

Printed in the United States
200044BV00001B/34-84/A